My Piece of Happiness

PARTHIAN BOOKS

Lewis Davies was born in Penrhiwtyn.

His first novel *Work, Sex and Rugby* established Parthian Books in 1993. His other work includes *Tree of Crows* and two stage plays *My Piece of Happiness* and *Without Leave*, both produced by Made in Wales. He won the John Morgan Award for his travel book *Freeways a journey west on route 66* and The Rhys Davies Prize for *Mr.Roopratna's Chocolate*. He has also written for the HTV Drama *Nuts and Bolts* and was co-editor of the *Mama's Baby (Papa's Maybe* New Welsh Short Fiction Initiative.

Lewis Davies lives in Cardiff with Gillian Griffiths and their children Tai and Ela.

My Piece of Happiness

Lewis Davies

PARTHIAN BOOKS

Parthian
The Old Surgery
Napier Street
Cardigan
SA43 1ED
www.parthianbooks.co.uk

First published in 2000.
This edition 2001.
Reprinted in 2002.
All rights reserved.
© Lewis Davies.
ISBN 1-902638-20-4

The publishers would like to thank the Arts Council of
Wales for financial support in the publication of this
volume.

Lewis Davies would like to thank
Dorien Thomas, James Westaway, Lowri Mae,
Sharon Morgan, David Middleton, Jeff Teare, Carolyn
Willitts, Ceri James, Dan Hyman,
Siân Bundy, Jo Nield, David Flinn, Rebecca Gould and
to say it is now, finally and completely,
in the novel.

Lewis Davies would also like to thank Gill Griffiths and
Norman Schwenk for generous help and advice in the
writing of this book.

Typeset in Galliard by NW.

Cover: Photography by Alessia Fanti & lloyd robson

Inside Artwork: Gods of Good Fortune
by Maldwyn Griffiths

Printed and bound by Colourbooks, Dublin 13,
Ireland.

With support from the Parthian Collective.

A CIP catalogue record for this book is available from
the British Library.

For Pete Grant,
Jeff Teare
&
Sylvia Mayne,
different reasons.

And, much too soon,
in fond memory of
James Westaway,
a fine actor and good friend.

'Hello, my friend.'

Sajid Malik

"Within the religions of Japan there are seven gods
of happiness or good fortune."

i

George looked carefully at the job advertisement. 'Earn Extra Cash. Paper Delivery. Hours Flexible, Easy Round.'

Maybe he could do it. If he could get four quid an hour it wouldn't be a bad rate. His eyes flicked over the other cards which hung in Collins' window. 'Child's bike, £15. Bedspread, hardly used. Bridesmaid dresses, set of three. Unwanted wedding. Lost. Black and white terrier. Answers to "Boy". Needs medication.'

The door to the shop opened. A woman in a washed brown coat pushed past George, her head bowed into the wind which was rushing along Corporation Road.

'Afternoon.'

The woman looked up but didn't smile.

'You still around then ?'

'Think so.'

Her head dipped. She pushed on.

George returned to the window, then checked his watch. Another twenty minutes and he would have to be at Andy's house. He straightened his collar, catching his reflection in the dirty glass. He had never been good at job interviews. A tin bell rang twice as he entered the shop.

A man stood behind a rack of brightly coloured chocolates and sweets. He looked up as George walked towards him. George knew the man by name but he had never been in the shop before.

'Collins, isn't it ?'

'Yeh, that's right mate. Can I help you ?'

'Enquiring about the job.'

'What job ?'

'The one in the window.'

'Paper deliverer ?' The man looked suspiciously at George. 'Aren't you a bit old for it ?' He had seen George around but had no idea who he was.

'Didn't say anything about age.'

'I know that. I was just expecting a... er younger man. School kid perhaps.'

George straightened his black tie. He could sense he was making Collins nervous. The newsagent shuffled a stack of magazines on the counter.

'It's been up there three weeks.'

Collins stopped shuffling the magazines and rearranged his chocolate display. He was sure one of his customers had told him a story about the man in front of him. It was a funny story but it had made him uneasy and now he couldn't remember what it was.

'So ?'

'You can't find anyone and I want to do it.'

'Deliver papers ?' Collins dropped a Mars bar behind the

counter. He hurriedly bent down to retrieve it but when he stood up again George was leaning over the counter, inches from his nose.

'Unless you have something else ?'

'No, that's it. Only job I've got left.' He backed away from the counter but continued talking. 'Papers come in on a Thursday morning. Round's along the Embankment, a few in the Close and most of the flats by the Gardens. You know the ones ?'

George nodded.

'About ninety houses in all, should take you about...'

'Three hours.'

'Yeh, about that.'

'And the pay ?'

'Ten quid.'

'Fifteen ?'

'I can't afford that. Ten's the rate.'

'Of course you can.'

Collins stared at George. Dark, fast-moving eyes stared back at him and smiled. What was that story ? 'Twelve, cash?' Collins clutched his magazines.

'Fine. Thursday afternoon then.' A bright smile cut across George's lips. He turned to leave.

'Er, your name ?'

'George.'

'Right, I'll expect to see you about two then ?'

George looked across at the newsagent. Collins edged

further back against the rows of cigarettes which hung above him.

'One more thing. I'll be bringing a friend along. Help me out a bit.'

'It's the same rate.'

'That's alright, we'll split it.'

George cranked his smile another tooth before turning for the door. He'd got the job.

Outside two cars edged forward, slowed by the lights. A woman pushed a pram along the pavement. Two kids, playing, shouting and pushing, ignoring George as they ran past. He pulled his coat tight around him, feeling its weight. The wind was strong but he could sense the spring rising with the big tides on the river. Saturday, the clocks would go forward.

ii

Andy is watching television. It is Sunday night. Andy watches television every Sunday night; Kaite claims he laughs louder on a Sunday night than any other night. Mike thinks he may laugh louder on a Wednesday night but not every Wednesday. Some Wednesdays Andy doesn't laugh at all.

Andy laughs at *Keeping up Appearances*, he laughs at *Eastenders* and *Coronation Street*, he laughs at *The Bill*. He laughs at *World in Action*, but he hates *The News*. *The News* curls his face into a tight twist of concern that becomes distress until Kaite or Mike or Angel change the channel. But usually he laughs a high spiralling laugh that rises out of his thin chest to splash around any room in which he happens to find himself.

Tonight being Sunday, he is in his own living room. A small but comfortable room, it bears the tawdry emblems of a small but comfortable income. Tonight being Sunday, he shares the room with Kaite but he could be sharing it with Mike or Angel or George. He likes them all and does not discriminate.

His latest burst of mirth has failed to evoke any response from Kaite, who sits across the room from Andy indifferently flicking through a magazine.

Mike had once asked Kaite her age, to which she replied, 'Mind your own fucking business,' in a tight Armagh accent that dissuaded him from ever asking again. She has lived in the city for three years and it suits her. Its tight impersonal streets, full of low-rent flats and split houses sate her need for constant, moving, change and easily smudges any traces of Ireland. Her accent remains but she has learned to use that. Everyone likes the Irish.

She looked up from her magazine as the credits flowed from the end of one programme into the next, but the change failed to hold her interest, and she returned to her shallow reading. Andy noticed her reaction, twisting his torso towards the settee, his mouth open as if to ask a question, but when her head dipped back he returned to view the screen.

The coloured television is accompanied by a hired video recorder with a fall of cassettes that spill over onto the carpet. The settee which shelters Kaite and her magazines looks clean and new, which it is. A smoked glass coffee-table separates the reader and viewer, supporting two mugs and an unused ashtray with *Gran Canaria* painted across the front in clear white letters. The walls are white; a bland print of a meadow in France is centred opposite Kaite, while threatening Andy is a hideous, framed wedding photograph of a couple in their late twenties, searching uncertainly for the camera and the future. A set of venetian blinds are drawn down to shield the room against neighbours and the glare of headlights, but Sunday nights in this area of the city are as quiet as the tide which slithers up the mud-banked river from the bay.

Kaite sleeps at Andy's house at least three, sometimes four, nights a week. It is a small bungalow, but the weathered tile roof shrouds three bedrooms. She has been sleeping at Andy's since she first arrived in the city. On the nights she's not at Andy's she returns to the flat she is briefly renting off Corporation Road, or on the Park, or near the Spar. She is always moving. It is a passion she feeds every five or six months, when she decides her flat is too dark or damp or close to the by-pass or the river or the park. Andy's place is the only constant in her itinerant new life in the city, and she loves him for it.

Tonight she is returning to her own flat, which is temporarily on the third floor of a Victorian terrace above Merches Gardens. Her last flat had boasted a back garden overlooking the park, but the school holidays had provoked a virulent rash of children that played and fought its way late into the long Summer evenings. The new flat had attracted her with a view over the slate rooftops to the river, but once the leaves had fallen from the high sycamores she could see the brewery and in the mornings a thick sweet smell of brown sugar and yeast settled over the flat like a veil.

Kaite dropped her magazine onto the pile which sprawled out across the settee and looked languidly up at the clock on the wall.

'Almost six now, Andy.'

There was a tired boredom in her voice from the flow of her reading but Andy didn't notice as he swung his head away from the screen. He looked at her expectantly, urging her to continue, which she did after allowing him enough time to reply.

'George will be here at six.' Andy's face immediately broadened into a smile which cracked into a stifled laugh followed by a twist of his neck. Kaite smiled at the reaction, pausing before she continued.

'You like George, don't you ? You like his cooking.' She lowered her voice closer to herself, 'Can't think why, fifty-nine varieties of meatballs with beans and potatoes.' She looked at Andy carefully, willing him to answer but her confidence in the one-sided conversation had waned.

Andy returned his attention to the television, tiring quickly of the sounds in Kaite's voice. His head moved, slipping towards his shoulder but he was only following the flickering colours of the screen. Kaite turned away, sensing she was again filling time.

She pushed herself up from the settee and walked over to Andy. She was a big woman and Mike would not have been alone trying to guess her age, which could be thirty or forty. Standing above Andy, she caught the question in his eyes as he looked up at her. She bent over, kissing him gently on the crown of his head before he brushed her away. Laughter comes quietly to her features.

Her thoughts were cut by the sharp trio of notes which announced the doorbell. Andy shivered with the noise and slipped lower into his armchair. A red belt stretched across his waist tightened further as it held onto its captive.

Sounds of a greeting drifted in from the passageway before George appeared in the doorway. Andy's face fired in enthusiasm as George lifted his arms in greeting.

'Awright, Andy ? How've you been, mate ?' George walked into the room and found a space on the settee between the cushions and the magazines. Kaite walked on into the kitchen.

Andy began another cackle of laughter as his hand came up from his side to frantically brush his nose. The laughter fell away but he had slipped further down into his chair where his stomach bulged out under the constraint of the red belt.

'Do you want a cup of tea ?'

'Love one, Kaite, put one on for Andy here as well.'

'He just had one.'

'Just me then.'

Andy twisted his head back towards George.

'How's he been ?'

Kaite shouted in from the kitchen. Their speech cut quickly across Andy who tried to follow the sounds as they talked.

'He's been okay. We had a walk down to the pier this

afternoon. He got a bit cold in the end though, didn't you, Andy ?'

'How's his bowels been ?'

'He had a movement this morning but that's the first for three days. I've been feeding him prunes but they don't seem to have had much effect.'

Andy drifted between the speech and the flickering faces on the screen. Unconcerned. It's Sunday evening, soon he will be going out.

'I'll change him before tea now. Init, Andy ? Quick change and you'll be all set for tea.'

Kaite returned to the living room and passed George a cup of tea. She sat on the settee next to George.

'You had a good weekend ?'

'Yeh, awright, you know.'

'Go anywhere ?'

'Nah, couple pints in the pub on Saturday. Nothing special. Yourself ?'

'No. I was working yesterday as well. We went over the market, bought myself some cheap nylons.'

'Busy ?'

'Always is.'

'Keep meaning to go but I never get round to it.'

'You should take Andy one Saturday. He likes it.'

'Yeh, I will.'

A tight silence slipped uncomfortably into the room as the people who could speak thought of something else to say.

George took a drink from his tea. Kaite glanced at the screen. The pictures move.

'Well, I've got to be going. I'm off out tonight.' She was lying but it came naturally and was easier to say than that she was staying in alone with the television and a bottle of red wine. She didn't want George to know that. She picked her leather bag from the side of the settee before striding over to Andy.

'See you then, Andy.' Andy looked up as Kaite bent over and kissed him lightly on the top of his head.

'Have a good night then.'

She smiled at him before heading for the doorway. One night she would have to talk to George. Talk about that night in her flat on the park. It was just the one night but he couldn't act as if nothing had happened.

George waited for the door to slam.

'What's got into her then, Andy ? Something you said ?'

Andy smiled at him.

'Never mind, it's just me and you now. U'are, 'ave some tea.' He picked a plastic beaker from the table and poured some of his own tea into it. The mug had a funnel-shaped adaption which he inserted into the side of Andy's mouth. Andy's head tilted back as he began to swallow the tea. The gulps were hard and quick, his eyes swivelling from side to side, still watching the screen while watching George. A hard swallow was followed by a gulp and a harsh retching splutter as the flow of the tea overtook him. He dribbled tea back onto his jumper.

'Shit, sorry, Andy, a bit fast for you there, was it ?' George hurriedly wiped the spilt tea further into Andy's jumper with a towel that was kept for the purpose, stuffed down the side of his armchair.

'Bit slower this time, is it ?' George re-inserted the cup carefully, watching how Andy reacted. Andy had been here before. He allowed the funnel to slip easily back into the side of his mouth.

'Chapel tonight, Andy. Fancy a bit of singing ?'

He paused but knew there wasn't going to be a reply from Andy whose attention was edged between the screen and the dribbling mug of tea.

'Anyway, finish your tea.' He allowed Andy the opportunity of one more swallow before he put the mug back on the coffee-table and removed the now sodden towel which he had left around Andy's neck as a bib.

'C'mon then, Andy.' He stood up and positioned himself on Andy's right side, before bending over to unbuckle the belt at his waist. He placed one hand behind Andy's back, his fingers curving around to grip onto his chest. He manoeuvred his other hand under Andy's knees as he bent lower, before straightening his back in one clean movement which lifted Andy out of his chair.

'There you are Andy, quick change. Then we'll smarten you up a bit.'

He handled Andy's weight with ease as he walked across

the room and out into the corridor towards Andy's bedroom beyond.

♦ ♦ ♦

Hotei

Sean is watching a screen. A screen that flickers light, bathing his pale features in shadows of black and white. The screen cackles and splutters through a vision of static but there is no sound, only light touching Sean and the faded brown armchair which surrounds him. Faint lines trammel through the light, reaching out as if to caress, but his face remains impassive and pale. A peel of laughter cuts in from the street beyond. A splash of moving headlights, then nothing. Only Sean staring into a screen of static from which there is no sound, only shadows of black and white, splintered shadows across his easy features.

♦ ♦ ♦

iii

The lounge bar of The Inn on the River is as slow as the water which slides slovenly between the festering mud-banks down to the Bay. Steve, the English landlord, argues with a frame of snooker on a portable tv, balanced for the evening on a stool stolen from the bar.

Andy and George were his only customers. The public bar was a slice more lively but his daughter covered the diehards who had braved the March rain for the comfort or escape of an establishment which had grown into its inevitable local name as The Pub on the Mud. Steve was content not to disturb her. He looked over at the odd couple ensconced in the far corner. Another pint, he guessed, and they would be heading home. He knew Andy lived on the far side of the Embankment. Most of the regulars had known his father, Arthur Day. Captain Arthur they used to call him on account of an ugly green tub he insisted on calling a yacht. But George, no one seemed to know where George lived. Steve liked to know people but he couldn't quite put a handle to George and it disturbed him. He knew he wasn't local, not a docks boy, but he seemed to have been around for years. Everyone knew him. But the knowledge never ran very deep. George, yeh sure, tidy bloke, been around for years. Been around for years where ? Doing what ? Conversations with him rarely led below the superficialities which endeared him to everyone. He could talk, sure; but when you really listened, which was hard, George seldom offered any information on himself. He asked easy, subtle questions which people liked and then he listened. And he was good at it too; people told him their secrets before they knew his second name.

Steve turned back to the tv as the frame petered out. He jabbed at the remote control with a chubby forefinger. The interior of a packed church appeared on the screen. He watched the faces for a while, full healthy white faces concentrating hard on the words. He pushed again. A long flowing shot of a green mountainside cutting to a rushing waterfall and Harry Secombe mouthing more words. Another fat white face. He flicked again but he knew the offering was going to be in Welsh.

'Shit.' He promised himself once again to turn the television aerial south across the channel the next time he forced himself up the fire escape.

'Two pints of dark, Steven.' George smiled across the bar.

'Yeh, sure, George, didn't see you creep up on me then.'

George just smiled as he passed two drained glasses across the bar.

Steve smiled back as he began to fill the first glass. That's another thing he thought, he always calls me bloody Steven.

Not even my mother calls me Steven. Was he shorter than he remembered ? He looked at George. His hair was shaved close to his scalp, black running to grey, but a vicious stubble still pushed sharp dark bristles through skin pulled taut across his face. His nose looked like it had been broken a couple of times. He was dressed for a dry Sunday. A starched white shirt and a black v-neck jumper covered a hard frame with bony jutting shoulders and long taut arms tapering to knuckle-filled hands that looked as if they could strangle a horse. A black tie added a veneer of severity to his features which they didn't need.

One of the regulars had claimed he'd seen him box back in the early 'seventies. There was something familiar about his style. Steve guessed he would have been a middleweight. One of those bastards who had been kicked in the face by life too many times to count but still had enough teeth to crack a smile.

If only he knew his surname. But it's not something you can come straight out and ask. Not to George.

'Not many in tonight, Steven ?'

'No, Sundays. They're all watching videos and the rain probably persuaded the regulars to stay in and watch the snooker.'

'Like yourself.' George nodded towards the portable.

'Don't know why I bother, they're all percentage players now.'

'You play a bit, I hear.'

'Yes.' Steve straightened himself with a flush of vanity; he must have heard about the team. 'Now and again down the Star, we're in the County League, not doing too bad this year.'

'Strong competition ?'

'Oh, you know, across the city. If we take the League we'll go to the regional finals.' He passed the second glass over to George. 'Two fifty-six.'

George immediately passed over a handful of coins that Steve knew before he counted would require no change.

'Well, best of luck. Guess I'll hear more about it.'

Steve turned to open the till still thinking about the match Wednesday night which would be crucial if they were to make the regionals.

George returned to his seat next to Andy who was sitting bolt upright in a formidable looking wheelchair. His thin body was enveloped by a Barbour jacket at least two sizes too big for him. It was partly undone at the collar, revealing a hand-towel which was serving as a discreet bib. The jacket glistened from the rain that had caught Andy and George on their way back from The Mission.

Andy was impatient for his beer and articulated a low moan which prompted George to offer him a drink from Andy's own plastic beaker. Andy tilted his head as he drank, swallowing in hard fast bursts as if trying to increase the dribble from the funnel. George steadied the flow, allowing

Andy to finish half the beer before relaxing back into his seat.

'What did you think of the sermon tonight then, Andy ?' His voice had a gently rhetorical edge. He knew he had to talk to himself but still allowed Andy time to absorb the question.

'He certainly livened the place up. The old folks loved that, a bit of hell and damnation.' George looked across at his companion to see if he was listening but Andy was concentrating on the empty lounge. Reassured, he resumed speaking to his audience of one.

'Everyone's frightened of death see, Andy. Frightened of something we don't understand.' George considered the claim to himself. 'You're not frightened of death though, are you ? You must have seen it once. It was after you then, what was it like Andy ?'

There was no darkness in his voice, just a simple question. He looked into Andy's face as if expecting an answer but there was nothing which suggested comprehension.

He swallowed, quickly and without thought, a quarter of his beer.

'You enjoyed the singing, didn't you ?' There was an easier, lighter vein to his voice but it was narrow and withering.

'Yes, of course you did. And Mr Philips gives you a mint every week. You know Mr Philips, don't you ? The guy who smells of tobacco. His son died, see, Andrew, he was a bit like you.'

Andy turned to face George but it was only to gauge the chance of another drink from the beaker. 'Slow down there, Andrew.' George raised the beaker to Andy's mouth, lowering his voice to continue the conversation with himself.

'In fact he was a lot like you, but he didn't survive. He wasn't as strong as you, see, Andrew, not a fighter. You're a fighter, would have gone into the ring, I'm sure of it. I can see you now.' His voice rose as if consumed by enthusiasm. 'A middleweight, Andy Day the docks destroyer, that would have been you. Might even have given me a going over.'

Andy turned away from George scanning the lounge.

'Your father always wanted a fighter. He got one alright.'

George followed Andy's face closely as he spoke in a precise deliberate summary. He finished the remaining three-quarters of his pint in two swallows, placing the glass carefully back on the table.

'Do you remember your Dad ? Used to take you out on his boat every Summer. The one with the big blue sail ? There's a picture of you in the album, strapped to the back, Andrew out in the Channel for a day with his Dad, July '68. Remember that ? And then he used to take you back to the hospital where you spent the remaining three hundred and sixty-four. Couldn't cope, could he ? Too much for your poor old Dad, weren't you, he needed a fighter.' George's voice thinned to a whisper as he finished his thoughts. Andy paid no attention but his face burst into a smile which deepened to a loud chuckle. George looked up to scan the lounge. A man had entered the bar; his skin glistened black, perhaps purple in the shaded light.

'Who's there, Andrew ? It's Patrick, is it ? You saw Patrick come in did you ? Did he see you ?'

Patrick stood at the bar facing away from them. He waited for his beer then began to walk away before he noticed Andy. He waved easily as if to apologise. Andy's grin broke into a laugh again as he approached.

Patrick burst into greeting as he neared the table. 'Andy mun, how are you, son ?' He spoke with a jocular voice, jarring with the obvious sobriety of its owner. 'George got you out drinking again, has he ? You're a devil, mind, aren't you? Out on the piss every night.' As he spoke he lowered his face to Andy's level and smiled. Andy began laughing again.'I bet you been up town chasing the women, haven't you ? You dirty bugger, I know what you're like, what a life, aye.' He shook his head and winked wildly to end the conversation. Andy laughed, his head swinging with the effort.

As Patrick turned to George his voice switched to an impossibly deep, grave tenor. Although he waited for it, the change always surprised George.

'How's he been ?'

'Fine, Patrick. We've just been down the chapel for a bit of singing.'

'Been down the chapel, 'ave you ? A bit of singing, is it ?

Great mun, give it a bit of hwyl, I hope ? I know what you're like, aye.' He added emphasis to his words by shaking his head in front of Andy's face. Andy's voice rose into a loud giggle that pushed out at the room. Patrick continued to smile at him, absorbing Andy's response before turning to George.

'Get the lad a drink, George.' He pushed a fiver across the table.

'You 'ave another drink, Andy. Don't get too drunk, mind. I know what you're like. A proper boozer given the chance. Lucky George is here to look after you.' He shook his head in front of Andy's face again, prompting another flow of laughter.

'See you, George.'

'Cheers, Patrick.'

Andy continued to laugh freely, throwing his head back in the process. Patrick headed through to the warmth of the bar. George watched him leave before turning to Andy.

'He's a good lad, Patrick, you like him don't you ? He's even bought you a drink.' He waved the note in his hand. 'We'll get a couple out of this ?'

Andy looked past him, towards the bar where a rise of voices welcomed Patrick.

'It's more than most of the bastards out there would give you. If you'd been a cute bloody donkey you'd have been fine. Give millions to bloody animal charities but next to fuck-all to you.' He paused, winding himself up. 'Never mind, you've got your own place now and no bugger's going to take it away from you.' George pushed himself up from the table, picking up the two glasses, but was called back by a low questioning moan from Andy whose face was contorted in a grimace.

'Don't worry, Andy. I'll get you a drink now.'

Andy continued his moan. The promise drained away while George ventured to the bar and returned with refilled glasses.

'Here you are, Andy.' He poured half a pint of dark into Andy's beaker, then inserted the funnel into the side of Andy's mouth.

Andy forced two swallows, then spluttered a mouthful out onto his jacket, intent on continuing his plea.

'You don't want to go yet, Andy. We haven't been in long.' He looked hopefully at Andy who increased the pitch of his moan, a dull insistent pulse that began to fill the lounge.

'There's nothing to do in the house mun, only watch the bloody tv. Look, I've just got another round in for us.'

Andy climbed to another pitch as he forced his torso out of the wheelchair, arching his spine backwards. His right foot, which had slipped from its strapping, rose sharply to kick the table. The table flicked over, spinning glasses and beer-mats to the floor. George caught one but the other spiralled out, first bouncing then shattering on the stained carpet.

'C'mon Andrew, there was no need for that. Look what you've done now ? Patrick just bought you that. I'll take you home but you could have waited until we finished our drinks.'

George was picking the pieces from the floor when Steve's daughter arrived with a bucket and mop.

'Sorry about this, he just got a bit excited, that's all.'

'That's alright, George, don't worry about it. You should see some of the stuff I have to clear up from here. If they were all as well-behaved as Andy we'd have no trouble.'

'Thanks, love.'

The thin rain had swept on, across the city, running to the low hills which welcomed it to the north. George pushed Andy silently along the Embankment. A single taxi rushed back to the offers of St. Mary's Street, its white light blinking for a fare. The streets brushed clear of people; even Malik's Discount Market had closed early to commerce. Sunday night, the night they shut the shops.

An hour later the screen in Andy's house flickered across the room. George lay curled up on the settee, his shoes discarded on the floor. He snored fitfully but didn't disturb Andy who was absorbed by the light and motion pushing out, clawing for attention. He was warm and dry and relieved to be out of the wheelchair. His home hugged him in its quiet comfort and changing faces that fed and clothed him like they had always done. It didn't help to get too close to anyone; one day they were there, part of everything; the next, gone through the door that led to the outside and they never reappeared. But tonight he was warm and full and content to watch and listen to the images on the screen.

iv

Merches Gardens was waiting for summer. Early Edwards had discarded egg yolk petals. A copse of false cherries splashed colour at the edges of the bowling green, the grass waiting for a cut before white-clad pensioners began the new league. Ruffian starlings picked through a barren rose-bed, ignoring a flock of young mothers chatting easily beside a paint-blistered bench. The mothers, rocking prams, in turn ignored a chubby man who sat alone on a bench under the shade of a fine chestnut. The tree was thick with fresh green leaves and white pyramid flowers that showered the man with petals when the wind skipped through the park.

Sean was counting. He counted with a careful assiduity the number of papers he had forgotten to deliver. The papers disturbed him; there were too many in the rough cloth sack that he had carried to the bench. He counted the papers as if not satisfied with his last result. Then hopefully he counted them again. There were always too many papers in the bag which carried his name in smudged marker letters.

He was a big man, heavy, with a boyish face that contorted into a parody of concentration as he counted. Even while sitting he looked ungainly, and when he walked he ambled as if unsure of his weight as he lumbered forward, smile first.

Restless with his calculations, he looked around the park. Passing over the mothers, he recognized a figure who entered through the far gate that led in from Corporation Road. His face immediately lost its painful concentration and broke into a broad grin. He waved a flat heavy hand towards George.

'Awright ?'

'Yeh.'

'Finished ?' George had joined Sean on the bench. He pushed his feet out, stretching back as he asked Sean, short, easy questions.

'Yes, George.'

'Quick this week ?'

Sean nodded, fingering his paper-sack.

'You got any left ?'

Sean nodded again, slowly, his eyes staring at his feet.

'How many ?'

Sean looked at him, waiting, checking his answer to himself before replying.

'Twelve, I've got twelve left. I had forty-five to start with George. Now I've got twelve.' Once started, Sean added extra words to any answer as if to emphasize its validity.

'We've got fifteen then because I've got three.'

'I didn't miss any out, George.'

'Yeh ?'

'I delivered them all.'

'Why do you think we've got papers over then ?'

Sean looked hopefully at George, shuffling his feet on the paint-dashed concrete. George waited.

'I don't know, George. I've got twelve and you've got three, that's fifteen.' There was a deliberate slowness to his maths, as if hoping the answer would have time to present itself. 'Why do you think we've got fifteen over, George ?'

'Did you do all the flats ?'

'All of them, George.'

'What about the Close ?'

'Did that, George.'

'Well, we've got fifteen left. Are you sure you didn't miss any out ?' There was a gentle note of teasing in his voice that Sean missed completely.

'I didn't, George. I delivered all mine, I wouldn't miss any out, George. I counted them all.' There was a desperate conviction to his claim.

'You counted them all ?'

'I did, George, all of them, all the houses on my side.'

'You sure ?'

'Even down the Close, George. Nine houses.'

George waited while Sean wrestled with a logic that always defeated him.

'Perhaps Collins gave us too many then ?'

'Yes, George.' Sean seized on the suggestion. 'He must

'ave. That's what he did, because I didn't miss any. I counted all mine.'

'We'll just have to tell him then, won't we ?'

'Yes, George.' His confidence in the solution wavered before he added. 'You'll tell, won't you ? You'll tell Mr Collins ?'

George's face broadened into a smile, his stubble rising over his jaw.

'Yeh, I'll tell him. Collins never could count, could he ?' He nudged Sean with his elbow.

'No, never could count, could old Collins. Everyone knows that.'

'But don't tell him, aye ?'

'No, George. No. I wouldn't do that George. I wouldn't tell him that.'

One of the mothers broke away from the flock and smiled unsurely at the paper deliverers as she walked past pushing an ugly kid in a stroller. George looked at the youngster; he was thin with pale, white skin. The people looked ill in this part of the city. It was as if all the weak people sank to the bottom and swilled around on a bad diet bought with pennies.

'Afternoon.'

She hurried on. Sean slowly counted his papers again. The park noticed nothing.

'We've always got papers over, George.'

'Aye I know that.'

Sean closed his bag. The papers are gone for now.

'Mrs Eynon said hello to me, George.'

'Did she invite you in for tea ?'

'I didn't go in this time, George. I know we've got to finish. I got to get home by six.'

'Your mother will be expecting you.' The last time Mrs Eynon had invited him in for tea George had spent an hour scouring the estate for any sign of Sean. He was just about to call the police when Sean padded up with half a packet of custard creams. A present from Mrs Eynon.

'She will, George. She gets worried when I'm not home.'

'How's your mother, Sean ?'

'She's fine, George.' Sean paused, reaching back. 'The doctor came on Saturday night.'

'He did ?'

'Yeh. But Mam's alright now. She was out of bed again yesterday.'

'Is the nurse still coming in the mornings ?'

'Yes, she still comes to get Mam up. She's lovely, Aunty Margaret.'

'How's your Dad ?'

Sean's face shone with excitement as he began to talk about his Dad. 'He's great. He took me to the football on Saturday, but we lost.'

'Good game ?'

'Yes, George, good game, but we lost. Dad wasn't very happy on Sunday. Told me to keep out of his way because of his head. I think he'd been drinking.'

'Your Dad likes a drink, does he ?'

'Sometimes, George, he likes it so much when we win he has to stay out. He sends me home in a taxi.'

'On your own ?'

'My mother doesn't like that though. She doesn't like him staying out on his own.'

'He took you home Saturday though ?'

'Yes. He said mam wasn't very well. And then the doctor came. He's like that, my Dad, he knows things.'

'Aye, he's quite a character, your Dad. And your mother's alright now ?' George tried hard to pull some confidence into his voice.

'Yes, she's fine.'

George held his words but knew that he had to go through with a decision he had already made.

'Sean, about your mother ?'

'Yes ?'

'She's very ill.'

'I know that. The doctor came. Mam said she'd be alright now.' There was a certainty in his voice that disturbed George.

'Sometimes, when people are ill, they don't get better.'

'Yes, I know that, George, but my mother will. She's my mother.'

George shuffled on the bench, pushing his back hard up against the wooden slats. Sean's absolute belief frustrated him, but he knew he couldn't be brutal.

'It's one thing to believe in certain things, but sometimes everything you believe can't be true. You can't help some things, can't do anything about them... beyond control. Even the doctors... Like your mother, Sean.'

'Yes, George.' Sean's eyes eagerly took his friends, willing to believe anything they were told.

'How's the centre ?' His words bit into him as he gave up.

'It's good, George. I'm learning everything there.'

'Aye.' He drifted.

'Mr Test thinks I'm doing really well.'

'He should know.'

'He says when I have my report, like, it'll be good.'

'You still making more friends there ?'

'Yeh, lots of them.'

George nodded his head, folding his fingers back into fists; he followed the lines on his hands as they cracked across his skin.

'Some I don't like though. Some are stupid.'

'You get them like that.' George's fingers flared out before he closed his fist again. Exercising.

Sean half-formed a word in his mouth before swallowing it back. The words stuck again. He tried turning the words in his mind before committing them to speech. They are slippery and he cannot hold them.

'Go on. What are you going to say ?'

'Nothing.'

'Go on mun. What were you going to say ?'

'I've got a girlfriend.'

"Ave you ?' George happily relaxed away from the health of Sean's mother.

'I have. Her name's Sarah Evans.' His voice was thick with pride.

'Sarah.' George paused, trying to fix the name in his mind. 'Nice name.'

Sean clapped his hands together tightly, squeezing them with excitement.

'Well ?'

'What, George ?'

'Where did you meet her then ?'

'I met her at the Centre. She's lovely.'

'I'm sure she is.'

'She's twenty-three.'

'Yeh. How long have you known her then ?'

'She's been there before me. Like a couple of years, I think. But we're going out now.'

'Am I going to meet her then ?'

'I dunno. I only see her at the Centre. You could call over, George. If you like.'

'Yeh, perhaps I will.'

'Wednesday. When we go on the bus.'

'Why don't you take her out on the weekend then ?'

Sean's face creased with frustration. 'Her mother won't

let her.'

'Aw c'mon. I'm sure she will.'

'No she won't. She's only allowed to the Centre.'

'You sure ?'

'Yeh, I'm sure, George. Sarah told me. Her mother takes her everywhere at the weekends.'

George waited for a way forward. Thinking. Sean kicked his shoes into the concrete.

'Do you want to take her out on the weekend ?'

'She won't be allowed. I just told you that.'

'But if she were ?'

'I'd love to, George, course I would.' He stuttered, gauging the possibilities. 'Where could I take her ?'

'What you doing a week Saturday ?'

'Football's over, George. But she's not allowed.'

'I tell you what. I'll have a word with Mr Test at the Centre and I'll see if I can persuade him to talk to her mother.'

'Where can I take her, George ?' There was a crest of panic rising in his voice.

'Don't worry about that. I'll take you both out in my car.'

'That would be great, George.' The panic fell away to excitement.

'What's her name again ?'

'I told you, Sarah Evans.'

'I know but I forgot. I'm useless with names.'

'Would you really take us out ?'

'Yeh sure. If I can.'

'You won't forget ?'

'No.'

'Saturday then.'

'Well don't get your hopes up but I'll see what I can do.'

'I won't, George. That would be great that though. In your car. The yellow one, right ?'

'Aye, the yellow one.'

'Saturday.'

'Week Saturday.'

'Yeh.'

'I'll talk to Mr Test.'

'And her mother ?'

'Mr Test will.'

'Not this Saturday, next Saturday.'

George pushed himself to his feet. More children had filtered into the park. They ran in circles, chasing the air. The young mothers had left. Sean looked out at the grass. His face beamed. George waited for him to stand but had to prompt him.

'You ready ?'

'What for ?'

'To go home, or your mother will be wondering where you are.'

'Yeh, sure, George.' He dropped his paper-sack as he stood and stumbled to pick it up again. When he straightened he looked down at George, waiting. He was five inches taller, his huge chest, rising and falling in excitement, holding up big, heavy shoulders.

'Give me your papers.'

Sean passed him the twelve papers out of the bag. His eyes fell as he remembered he must have missed houses. George folded them with his own and then dropped them into a wire bin which stood, full of crisp packets and plastic bottles, at the end of the bench.

The papers sank into the rubbish.

'Don't want Collins to think we didn't deliver them all, do we ?' He smiled at Sean whose eyes remained on the papers in the bin.

◆ ◆ ◆

Fukorokuju

Sean is watching a screen. A screen that flickers out to him, bathing his pale easy features in splintered shadows of black and white. The screen speaks to him; words and phrases, whole sentences break their way through a vision of static. The lights suggest shapes. Light fingers, pressing. Moving shapes, figures of people just behind the blurred curtain of black and white. Voices stir from the street beyond.

A discarded wrap of chip-paper, stained with grease and red sauce, lies used and silent on the floor; a mug of tea cools by the side of his chair. The room brushed by moving headlights.

Only Sean, staring into a screen of static, listening to the words that reach out and touch him: phrases, whole sentences, shadows moving behind the splintered curtain of black and white.

◆ ◆ ◆

v

Ayoung woman looks into a dressing-table mirror. Her face flares back balancing between anger and frustration. Red smears colour her lips, smudging around the corners of her mouth where her hand has not been steady enough to hold a line. Her eyes rise high as she tries to add dark lines to her eyelashes. Her hand held still, not daring to move.

'Sarah ?'

The voice came from deep within the house. Below the stairs. The young woman leaned closer to the mirror, trying not to listen as the footsteps climbed the stairs.

'Sarah.' Another call, sweeter this time, nearer. She tried again with the eyeliner.

'Sarah, are you ready yet ?' Her mother's face appeared at the doorway.

'No, not yet.'

'Sarah, the gentlemen will be here at twelve.' Her mother was tall and elegant but Sarah did not see her that way.

'I'm not ready yet.'

'It's not polite to keep them waiting.'

'Sean don't mind waiting.'

'That's not the point.' Her mother pulled the curtains

back from the window and the easy, thin light of early Summer filled the room.

'He's always late anyway.' Sarah's face was lost in the mirror.

'How do you know that ?'

Sarah shrugged her shoulders.

'Sarah ?'

'He just is. He's always last. Swimming, dinner time. Everything.'

'Perhaps today he'll be on time.'

Sarah screamed at the mirror, filling the room with her frustration. Her mother adjusted the curtains.

'Shall I help you, Sarah ?'

'I can do it.'

'Just take your time. It'll come.'

Sarah dropped the eye-liner to the table. It bounced hard on the glass surface, spun, then stopped. She picked up the lipstick. Her mother pulled away from the window.

'Is Sean new to the Centre ?'

'He's been there a year.'

'You've never mentioned him before.'

'I haven't been seeing him before, have I ?'

'You should have told me about him.'

'Why ?'

'You know your father doesn't like surprises.'

'He's okay, Sean. Dad'll like him. He's got a job.'

'A job ?'

'He has. He delivers papers. Him and Mr Rees.'

'I thought Mr Rees worked at the Centre ?'

'No. He delivers papers with Sean. Every Thursday.' Sarah's face checked the facts. There was something missing. She was sure. 'I think he might have another job as well.'

'I hope so.'

Sarah leaned closer to the mirror, her nose almost touching the glass. She brushed her lips once with her lipstick, then sat back, satisfied.

'Where are they taking me ?' She scratched at the top of the table as she talked, her hands knocking over sprays and lacquers.

'I told you. It's a surprise.'

'I want to go to the beach.' Her fingers grasped at the brush.

'It's too cold for the beach.'

'The beach next week then.'

'Next week, is it ?'

'He's my boyfriend. I like him.' Her cheeks coloured with pride as she formed the word. Her mother pulled further away from the table.

'Yes, we'll see.'

'I can have a boyfriend, can't I ?' Her question caught her mother, holding her in the spell of the mirror.

'You know you can, Sarah.'

'And Dad won't mind ?'

'You've had a boyfriend before.'

'I've never been out before.'

'You've never asked.' Her mother wanted to leave the conversation but Sarah was calm now.

'Dad would have said no.'

'You're older now.'

'Does that make a difference ?'

'Of course it does.'

'How ?'

'You can do other things. Grown up things.'

'Like what ?'

Her mother stared out of the window, wishing the morning would move forward.

'You're going out on on your own on a Saturday afternoon. That's what you can do.'

'Is that all ?'

'Isn't that enough ?'

'I want to do more.' She slammed her left hand down hard onto the table.

'But this is a new thing for you. You can't do it all at once.'

'I'm old enough.'

'I've told you that but there's no rush.'

Sarah's voice raced on, her hands pulling a brush hard through her hair. Her eyes on fire in the glass.

'I want to go out every night and...'

'You'll be able to see him again.' The words ended the race.

'I will ?' She got up from the chair.

'Yes. If you like him.'

'I like him a lot.' She hugged her mother, loving the words. 'He's my boyfriend. You had a boyfriend didn't you?'

'Yes, once.'

'Is he still your boyfriend ?'

'He's your father.' The words stop Sarah. She can't find the meaning.

'Dad's your boyfriend ?'

'He is.'

'He's too old to be your boyfriend.'

'We've got older.'

'Nah, don't believe you.'

'When you get older, you get married.'

'I could get married.'

'Why would you want to do a thing like that ?'

'So I could live with someone.'

'You don't need to do that. You live with us.'

'Yeh, I could still get married and live with you.' She returned to the pool of the mirror.

'I'm not sure your father would be too keen on that idea.'

'But I'm older now.'

'You're always rushing into...' Her words were covered by bottles and sprays as they were pushed off the dressing table onto the floor. Sarah screamed.

'No, no, no.'

The words filled the room, then silence. Sarah's shoulder shook as tears began to come to her eyes.

'No.' She spoke the word quietly once more, wishing she hadn't said any of it. Her eyes found the scattered bottles on the floor. How can they be there ? Their place is on the table.

'Come here, Sarah.'

The young woman turned from the mirror, dark lines running from her eyes.

'You need to take your time a bit more.' Her voice flowed over her daughter as she brushed the smudges and lines away. Her hands worked quickly. A painted face. 'There.' She turned her daughter once more to the mirror. 'You look lovely, Sarah.'

vi

'You sure you said thirty-eight ?'

Sean just smiled back at him, his face filled with anticipation.

'Great car, George.'

George was fervently wishing he'd taken the exact address from Test. The clock had pushed past midday and they were the last quarter of the hour late. Fifteen minutes spent chasing a mobile address around the tree-lined roads of Llanishen. Number thirty-eight, Sean had insisted after sixty-eight turned into a Shell garage. Thirty-eight Larkspur Crescent only there didn't appear to be a Larkspur Crescent only a Larkspur Road and maybe a Drive the far side of the railway according to a pensioner at the Spar store. The yellow Horizon complained, refusing to change gear with any style. George had been intending to scrap the car for months. Selling it was out of the question. The tax-disc was only a month out of date but the insurance had lapsed at Christmas. He was planning it would last until the end of the Summer.

'Great car, George.'

'Yeh, sod the car, where's the bloody house ?' He'd never liked Llanishen.

'There's Sarah.' Sean pointed across the road to where a pair of women idled on the corner of Larkspur Crescent. He waved frantically across the car. George veered the car to the far side of the road, pulling up alongside the waiting mother and daughter. Sean stopped waving as Sarah's mother dipped towards the car. George lowered the window.

'Mrs Evans, my pleasure.' He offered his hand.

'Oh, hello. MrRees ?' She appeared nervous but was desperately trying to retain her composure.

George was surprised how attractive he found Mrs Evans. He was expecting an old woman in her fifties. He was right about her age but nothing else. She dressed with a style that came from money. Her daughter appeared cumbersome by her side, slightly fat with her hair pulled severely back and fastened. She was wearing a white flowery blouse and a tweed skirt.

Sarah waved shyly at Sean.

'Go on then, open the door for Sarah then.' He nudged Sean.

'Yeh, sorry, George.' Sean stumbled out of the car and very formally shook Mrs Evans's hand before opening the rear door for Sarah. He followed her in, slamming the door in enthusiasm.

'MrTest assured me you'd look after her.' She peered down dubiously at George, eyeing the rusting bodywork of his car as if in confirmation of his irresponsibility.

'No problem. Any particular time you'd like them back?'

She risked a look at Sean, trying to judge him.

'Perhaps three, three-thirty.'

'Fine.'

'Do you know where you're going ? I mean, where you are taking them ?'

'I thought the lakes at Cosmeston.'

Mrs Evans appeared to gauge this suggestion in her mind and, while finding no apparent fault in it, remained uneasy.

'You are experienced ? I mean you've done this sort of thing before ?'

'Been working for the service five years.'

George smiled up at her, nodding. What the hell was Test up to ? He was supposed to have explained the situation.

'I guess you'll be alright.' She smiled weakly at George. He would have to do.

She was still waving as he spun the car around and headed south.

vii

Cosmeston ripples with sunshine and the silent paddling of Coots that weave through the bullrushes, clinging to the shallow margins.

Sarah and Sean lingered on the edge of a grassy bank that dipped into the water on the far side of the lake. They had attracted a few curious glances as they strolled hand-in-hand along the path from the car-park. George had allowed them to walk ahead as he watched the birds in the reeds. A set of binoculars hung from his neck. He knew the lakes well. There was a rumour that a Water-Rail had been seen; there might even be a pair nesting.

Sean looked back along the path for George. Sarah clasped his hand and looked for the sun. They moved closer together as George reached them on the bank.

'Here we are then, folks, on the lakes. Like it here ?'

'Yeh, George. It's good.'

'I like the water, Mr Rees.'

'Call me George, mun, love. I don't know who Mr Rees is.'

Sarah dipped her head but Sean was listening to George. 'You're Mr Rees.'

'I know that. What do you call me ?'

'George.'

'There you are then.'

Sarah smiled at him. 'Nice of you to bring us, George.'

She held the last word, emphasising it.

'Nice to be out on a Saturday.' George looked out across the lake through his binoculars

Sean was enjoying himself, he liked talking. 'I like to go to the football on a Saturday. My Dad takes me.' He looked at Sarah and George, waiting.

'I thought the season had finished ?'

'It has now, George. But next year perhaps we can all go to the football ?'

Sarah smiled at him but Sean was oblivious to anything but holding her hand.

'Are you going to take us out every Saturday, Mr Rees ?'

'You won't want to come with me every week, I'm sure.'

'Why, George ?'

'I don't want to be with me every Saturday, but I ain't got no choice in the matter.'

'What do you mean, George ?'

'You'll be wanting to go out, on your own and things.' His hands moved, trying to suggest a wider world, Saturday and time together.

'My mother wouldn't like that, Mr Rees, you'll have to come too.'

'Aren't we thinking a bit much here, good people ? We're out today. Now.'

A silence covered them.

Dragonflies flirted with the shimmering surface of the water, hovering, then skipping away.

'It's lovely, Mr Rees. The water. Very nice of you to bring us, Mr Rees.'

'Call him George, Sarah.'

Sarah turned sharply to Sean, eyes flaring.

'Never mind, you call me what you like. I'll answer to it.'

The voices of children, carried over the water, reached them from the playground near the car-park. A windscreen caught the sun, flashing. Sean shuffled, George looked out over the lake to the far bank.

'Are we going to eat now ?' Sean was happy that he had found words to say. Time for something else to happen now.

'Sure, if you want to. The sandwiches and stuff are in here.' George pulled a haversack from his shoulder. 'Are you hungry, Sarah ?'

She shrugged her shoulders. 'Sure, Mr Rees.'

He looked over again to the far bank where the reeds thickened around a stream which flowed into the lake. The Water-Rails might be nesting there. Moorhens edged out of the shallows. He turned his view to Sean and Sarah. They both smiled at him.

'I'll leave you to the food. I'm not that hungry yet, and someone told me there's grebes on the far side.' He pointed over the water. Sean and Sarah followed his hand, and then looked unsurely at each other.

'You'll be alright here, won't you ?' He watched Sarah's face closely, but she appeared unconcerned. 'No swimming now.'

'No, George, we wouldn't do that but what about your sandwiches ?'

'Don't worry about me. I'll have some when I get back. I'll be about an hour, right ?' He allowed his question to hang, hoping for a response.

'Okay, George. We'll stay right here.'

George was already moving away along the path. Sean began to shout after him. 'We won't go anywhere. We'll stay right here.'

George raised a hand above his head without turning around. Sean ran out of things to say and stopped shouting. He shuffled around, still holding Sarah's hand. She smiled confidently at him, but Sean is the first to speak.

'Do you want a sandwich ?'

'No.'

'George made them.'

'I'm not hungry.'

'Cheese and tomato.'

Sarah shook her head. 'We can eat later.'

'Yeh.' Sean seemed disappointed but placed the sandwiches back in the haversack. 'Do you like George ?' He spoke shyly, nervous of testing the approval of his friend.

'Yeh, he seems nice.' A confidence edged into Sarah's voice now that they were alone.

'He's my mate, George is, we work together on the papers. You know, my job I told you about ?'

'On a Thursday ?'

'That's the one. I get paid for it.'

'How much ?'

'Fifteen pounds.'

'Really ?'

'George says I don't even need to pay tax if I keep it quiet.'

'My dad pays tax.' A confidence filled her voice. She was out, on her own, on a Saturday afternoon talking to her boyfriend.

'I don't. I keep all my money. That's what George says.'

'Did you miss any out this week ?'

'Sssh mun. Someone might be listening.'

'Don't be silly.'

'I had nine left.'

'You must have missed some houses then.'

'I counted them all.'

'But you had some over.' She was concerned, which forced Sean to try harder to remember how he missed the houses. He had counted them all, he was sure.

'You won't tell George, will you ?' Sarah held her reply, teasing him. 'You won't ?'

'No, course not.'

'Cos I don't want to lose it.'

'I'm not going to tell anyone.' She smiled at Sean, who

tried to kiss her. He moved too quickly, clumsily missing the moment.

He turned away. 'Sorry.'

'What for ?'

'I don't know.'

'Put the rug down so we can sit on the grass.'

Sean looked at Sarah and then at the rug which filled the haversack, then at Sarah again.

'I'll put the rug down.'

He grabbed the rug from the haversack, unfolding it onto the grass, then he carefully pulled out the corners to flatten the creases. He stood back, watching as Sarah sat confidently in the middle of the rug. She kicked off her shoes, pushing out her stocking-covered toes. Sean watched.

'C'mon then.'

Sean looked at Sarah dumbly for a second before joining her on the rug. His arm drifted shyly around her shoulder. She turned and kissed him on the lips, responding to his arm with a hug of her own. They eased back onto the rug.

A blue-bottled emperor dragonfly dipped back out of the rushes, plying its angled path across the twenty-four lakes of its mind's eye. Near the lock, George watched a Little Grebe as it slipped under the water, the smallest three ripples breaking out for the shore.

♦ ♦ ♦

Jurojin

Sean is watching a screen. A screen that reaches out to him, bathing his pale easy features in splintered shadows of black and white. The screen speaks to him; words and phrases, whole sentences break their way from the moving shapes that hover and fade. The shapes have edges, forms, movements. Names call him from the street. A man speaks to him from the shadows, stumbles forward, smelling of cheap whisky and cigarettes.

'She's gone, son, it's just me and you now.'

The man stops but Sean doesn't turn. There is only Sean staring into a screen, listening to the words that reach out and touch him. Phrases, whole sentences that speak to him. Watching the shapes that have edges, movement, faces. Shapes that have moved from behind the curtain.

♦ ♦ ♦

viii

The hospital is a dank, rambling hulk, stranded on a hill by the ravages of penicillin. George could still count the rows of thin white young men facing the chill wind rushing in from the rising Channel. The walls seemed hollow, breathing, the building alive. Prefabs took root in the car-park and the playing fields, growing even as they rotted. The hospital festered, swelling with wings and corridors that clawed their way across the hill, leading to more paint-flaked wards where people could be forgotten for a lifetime, and were.

The air of futility disturbed George. The place had a simple function of containment. The waste cast away on the edge of a housing estate, fenced in by a dual-carriageway and a marsh, as if the site had been chosen for the defences. Keep the people out, the patients in.

Sure, there were escapes, but the patients were harmless; they only scared the shit out of everyone. The fear of the unknown. Severe, contorted faces, eyes seeing nothing. You couldn't talk to people like that. They couldn't understand language. They weren't normal.

George let himself into Ward III. The orderly at the desk had assured him Sean was fine. No, they hadn't been able to get him a room to himself, but Ward III was okay. One of the quieter wards. He would have got some sleep. How long was he staying ? George didn't know. A week, maybe longer. As soon as they could fix him up with a house. It wasn't that easy.

The ward was bare. The walls covered with flaking paint. A battered settee extended the length of the common room. A huge television played in the far corner. Another orderly watched it intently. He was the only one in the room interested in cricket. Other figures walked around, unconcerned as they ignored George, absorbed in their own interior world.

A man touched his arm. George hadn't noticed him sidle up behind. His face was young, innocently hopeful. His bony fingers clasped George's wrist, and he pointed. Out towards the world George had entered from. His eyes looked for a response, but George only released his fingers and shook his head. The boy looked away before drifting off further into the common room.

The futility. The lost people who waited on the ward for people who never came. Parents who had decided not to struggle, abandoning them to their own fate. Unable to bear the weight. And what was wrong with that ? George guessed he would have done the same. They just waited here, names. Names on a caseload. Social workers who only had time to discuss their case once a year. Time to tell a doctor there was no money in the budget; time to write that they would have to remain on the ward for another year. Next year there might be money for a service. Money for a few hours a week. Money to get them out of the ward.

George looked for someone to speak to. A group of nurses and orderlies gossiped over a cup and a fag, crammed around a table, suitably sheltered, in the ward office. There was a burst of harsh laughter as someone spewed a joke. Then one of the coterie noticed George.

'Can I 'elp you, mate ?' He didn't get up from his chair. Fingers grasping a fag.

'Sean Dent, I'm his keyworker.'

'Oh yeah, Sean.' He turned to his companions, spitting a whispered question.

George stood framed by the doorway; one of the nurses ran a glance over him cautiously.

'We think he's out in the garden.'

'Garden ?'

'Yeh, there's a garden at the back of the ward, through the common room, hang a right.'

George nodded. The man looked up, impatient for him to leave.

'How's he been ?'

'Fine, fine.'

'Settling in okay ?'

'Yeh.'

One of the nurses got up from her chair and pushed past George. 'See you later.'

'Sure. Give us a bell if you need me.'

The departing woman didn't even smile at George. He returned to the man answering his questions.

'Anything else ?'

'Anything else what ?'

'Has he been upset, nervous ? Other obvious signs of distress ?'

'How do I know, mate ? This isn't an observation unit, you know. What do you want, a progress report ?'

The group on the table sniggered to themselves.

George looked at the man, his fingers tensed, blood filled the tight skin on his face. The orderly turned away uneasily. One of his friends who had been playing cards on the table put his hand down.

'I'd better be going. Stores to finish.' He edged past George, eyes down.

'And me, Ron. See you later.' The orderly's last companion deserted him. The remaining occupant of the room looked at George and then picked up a newspaper from an empty chair and began to read.

George moved forward into the room. 'That progress report you mentioned, it might be extremely helpful.'

The man stared at his newspaper.

'Why don't you ask one of the staff nurses ?'

'Which one was that ?'

'She's not on at the moment. Another hour.'

'Right.' George looked around the small room. The

orderly shuffled in his seat, trying to forget George was there. George thought about leaving and then moved closer to the man, looking over his shoulder. 'Anything good in the paper?'

'What ?'

'Useful information, spiritual guidance on how to live life ?' His voice lightened but the orderly buried himself deeper in the useless news.

'It's all rubbish, mate.'

'Has it got a tv page ?'

'Yeh, they all have. Why ?'

'Sport ?'

'At the back.' He turned the newspaper to emphasize the point, his voice beginning to sound tense.

'Crossword any good ?'

'What you on about ?'

'Just passing time.'

'I told you where he is.'

George leaned close to the orderly, inches from his face. 'Do you enjoy your job ?'

'Hey.' The orderly struggled to his feet. He was taller than George, heavy but overweight.

George leaned closer still. 'Well ?'

'Who do you think you are ?'

'I told you, I'm his Keyworker, assessment officer, paper-deliverer, ex-boxer. Friend.'

'So ?'

'I expect a bit more co-operation from a fellow professional.'

'We can only do so much.' He was leaning away from George but George was following him.

'And I only have this amount of patience left.' His hand shot close to the man's eyes, finger and thumb threatening to close the air between them. This much left. This much.

The man pulled away from George, dropping his paper onto the table. 'I'll see if I can get one of the nurses to talk to you. I wasn't on when he was admitted.'

George relaxed back, smiling. 'That would be an excellent idea.' He caught the man's arm before he could leave the room.' And find out about his medication prescription while you are there. Stress can change his behaviour, awright ?' He allowed the man to shuffle out of the room.

George looked around the empty office. Tea congealed in plastic cups, cards face-up on the table, today's copy of *The Daily Mirror.*

ix

George walked on, through the common room. A cackle of laughter, strange uncontrolled laughter, bubbled up from a chair positioned alone in an annexe to the main room. An old man, bald as an egg, laughed all to himself, his eyes closed tight against a lifetime of blindness. George hurried on.

He forced open a red fire-door, which scraped across a grey concrete path that fringed the garden.

The garden was a quadrangle of green, mown grass. A few stunted rose bushes sheltered on the south-facing wall. A solitary child's swing with a red seat stood to one side. The grass under its arc was worn back to packed brown earth. Sean hung forward from the seat, head bowed, watching his feet as they pushed him backwards, then forwards, through a stunted arc.

'Hello.'

Sean looked up, immediately recognizing the voice.

'George,' he spluttered, 'George how...how are you here?'

'I'm here to see you, aren't I ?'

'George, to see me, you've come up to see me ?'

'Course I have.'

Sean beamed at him, his cheeks setting red.

'Thanks, George.'

'That's alright mun, you're my mate.'

Sean squinted at George, trying to determine if he was being teased.

'Really, George ?'

'Course.'

'I'm your mate too, George, honest I am. I'm you're mate on the papers, right ?'

'That's right.'

Sean looked away.

'I don't like it here, George.' He turned his head back down. A sobriety streaked through his voice. 'It's not nice.'

'No, I guess it's not.' George looked around him. He wanted the hospital to speak, laugh, curse, say anything, so he could react, but the walls remained implacably calm.

'I don't like it here.'

'You're okay though, aren't you ? No one's touched you or anything ?'

'Not nice, George. Not nice.' He dug the toe of his soiled trainers into the mud. 'Don't want to stay here long, George. Want to go back home ?'

'Can't go back home right now, Sean. You might have to stay here a few days.'

'Want to go home.' His head fell further.

George put his arm around the man's shoulder. 'Your Dad. Your Dad can't cope too well on his own. He's old, see, and he's missing your mother.'

Sean leaned into George, allowing the words to sink in, swallowing them as he moved forward in his mind.

'My mother, George, she's gone, hasn't she ? Gone.' There was a cut of despair in his voice that he didn't know how to hide. 'They said she was going to get better, George. They said, they promised. But she's not, is she, George ? She's not going to get any better ?'

'No, she's not. She can't get better now. You mother was very ill, in a lot of pain. You know that, don't you ?'

He nodded sullenly. 'She's out of pain now, George. My Dad said that.'

'He's right, Sean. The pain's over now. No more.' George held Sean's head, pulling him closer. He knew it was hard to gauge his friend's response to explanation.

Sean pulled away, holding himself steady. He had more questions.

'George ?'

'Aye ?'

'When people die, right. When they die, they're buried, right. In the churchyard like my Gran.'

George nodded.

'Are they putting Mam there ? In the churchyard ?' There was a faint surge of hope in his question.

'Yes, I think so.'

'Right.' He nodded to himself as if the answer confirmed his reasoning. He folded this information away as he thought of a way forward. 'George, has your mother ever died ?'

George caught himself pulling away as he stumbled with a half-answer. 'I'm not sure. Probably by now.'

'Did they put her in the churchyard ?'

'I like to think so, Sean. Somewhere warm by the sea perhaps.'

'You'd be upset too, wouldn't you ?'

George dug a bar of Galaxy out of his jacket pocket. He snapped it into pieces, offering one to Sean.

'Chocolate ?'

'Thank you, George.' He looked at the chocolate, unsure what to do with it.

'I don't think you'll have to stay long.'

Sean pulled his friend nearer, his eyes wide with concern. 'The people.' He waved his hand towards the quadrangle and the hospital beyond. 'They look at me, George, just stare. Don't say anything, then they laugh or scream, sometimes both.' He leaned closer, pulling George in, his eyes opening wide as if letting him into a huge secret. 'I think they're mad, George.'

'They're not mad, Sean.'

'They could be. You'd never know. Nutters.'

'Don't worry, they're fine, mate. Have another chocolate.'

Sean held the two soft squares of chocolate in his head, staring at them as if they were something special and unknown, a talisman. Knowing they were only squares of chocolate.

'Thank you, George.'

x

George stared down from the office into the car-locked back of the Team Headquarters. Water filled the holes in the tarmac, a brown muddy water that ruffled easily as a swirl of wind played chase with discarded cigarette wrappers around the wheels and hubcaps. His own Horizon looked comfortable parked near the back under a hedge of firs, its rust and general dishevelment in company with its corralled companions. Only an enormous blue Mercedes stood apart from the general air of secondhand pushing scrap. The Merc belonged to Mohan. Mohan was the landlord who rented the Victorian terrace at an exorbitant rate to the Team. He kept the best suite of offices for himself, entertaining friends, signing business, reading *The Times*. There was a framed picture of a town in the Punjab hanging above his desk, a town his father had abandoned in the 'fifties and he hadn't seen for fifteen years. It was better that way, at a distance. The dust and flies were the imagination, his memory the reality.

George sat behind one of the three desks that had been squeezed into the attic of the building. Mohan, as economical as ever, converted every floor, guessing correctly that the team would expand to fill any space offered. He was even furnishing the cellar as storage space. The Team was considering. There was money in the budget. Spillage money.

'It's almost two.'

George turned to acknowledge the pronouncement from Angel. She looked sharply at George to see if he was paying her attention, pausing from her constant pacing of the room. She was tall, thin and gave the impression that her body was constantly on the move; which it was, her actions, motions of perpetual decision. She checked her watch, her file, which she clasped jealously to her chest and then the clock on the wall. George watched her. He was intrigued by her restless, stuttering steps. He tried thinking of her in bed; did she move that much, thin arms wandering ? He had tried once, one boozy Friday evening when they had all gone out to The Albert. He had lingered with her on the way back to the office, and she had pulled him viciously towards her under the shelter of the bike-shed. It was too corny to laugh, but when it was getting serious, her thighs lifting easily up and apart, she had whispered, 'I'm married,' which he knew anyway, and eased him away. But George didn't give up that easily. The memory still gave him a rush of blood that lingered delicately, but it was only once. It could have been one of those things you try for the hell of it and let go.

'They promised they would be here by one.' Angel looked up at the clock. 'I suppose we should have expected it really, the day after the funeral.' She appeared to concede that this was an adequate excuse.

'They'll have a few things to think about.'

George turned to the source of the observation. A deteriorating grey man, bunkered between a filing cabinet and the far wall. George had half-forgotten he was there. A bust of Marx and a lonely poster of Nelson Mandela guarded him, twin icons of futility and hope that failed to protect him from the reality of the team and its endless, interminable problems. He fiddled with his pen, then his cuff-links.

'Still, it's almost an hour now,' insisted Angel. She checked her watch again as she continued to pace the room.

'It's always a difficult time.'

George returned to the view of the car-park.

Someone's hand appeared, disembodied, at the annexe door leading out into the car-park. The hand tapped twice before retreating into the shelter of the annexe. Then a lungful of smoke, coughing outward, raised a smile to George's face. Puff was at it again, taking her third fag-break of the afternoon, drawing deeply on a tarred packet of Regals. He could just see her feet on the doorstep smeared by the rain. She wasn't the only smoker in the Team, just the most committed. Puff had threatened the Union when the office was declared No Smoking. A threat which resulted in a Team secret ballot. A secret ballot to which George had secretly added fifteen No Smoking votes on a dark Wednesday evening when he had let himself in after hours. The result barred smoking by three votes. George was delighted, the majority of the voters angry at the unseen traitors in their ranks and cursing the part-timers.

The hand shot out again, flicking a butt onto the tarmac. George caught its last smudged flare before it soaked in the water. The door to the annexe closed. Give her twenty minutes, thought George. He was still smiling sourly to himself when one of the figures he had been waiting for, half-hidden under a red umbrella, crossed the tarmac and presented herself at the side entrance. His hopes had climbed to three visitors but they had never reached high enough to broker much disappointment.

'I think this is her now. No sign of Sean or his dad.'

'His father must be coming.'

'Doesn't look like it.'

'We can't get very far without him.'

'He's not with her.'

'I spoke to him yesterday morning.' Exasperation poured from Angel.

'What about Sean ?'

'I did try to insist that he should attend.'

'Just like the funeral.' George was as frustrated as Angel.

'They didn't think he needed to be there.'

'Or here by the looks of it.'

'It wasn't easy.'

'He should have attended.' George was emphatic.

'The funeral I can understand.' Test offered a few words as if he had to contribute something to the debate.

George turned to face him. 'Why ?'

'It can be upsetting.'

'It's a funeral.'

Angel looked at her colleagues uneasily. They were arguing already. George had a reputation for difficult meetings. This was going to be a long afternoon. 'I'll go and show her in.'

Test and George were left alone. George was still staring, eyes asking a question. Test shuffled nervously; he disliked meetings and was generally uneasy with people. The impending discourse had already unsettled him. He fervently hoped he could escape without expressing too many opinions. His own private nightmare hovered around the responsibility of a decision that was all his own.

He studied his files, trying to recall some details of the Dent family. Sean was easy, the big, lumbering lad who kept running away from the Centre. The police had been called twice. Missing persons. But Sean had only gone as far as the central bus station, where the drivers took him along to the lost property office. He could get on a bus but never had any money for the fare. He was too big to argue with, and all the buses eventually returned to the station. Sean caused the sort of problems you could easily laugh about.

'Do you know the family, George ?'

'Sort of, you know how it is.' George had returned to staring out of the window. 'The mother made all the decisions.'

'What about Mr Dent ?'

'He's alright. Nice enough bloke but he's been drunk for years.'

'It's always a shame.'

'Just another way out.' George brushed some dust from the arm of his jacket.

'And Mrs Grigeli is Sean's sister ?' He read as he spoke, trying to confirm his information, hoping his files would not let him down again.

'She's married with kids. I've only met her once or twice.'

'Older than Sean then ?'

'Five or six years probably.'

'And has she been supportive ?'

'She used to be more involved. Grew up with it all.'

'Have you spoken to her about the future ?'

'I don't really know her that well. Caught up with her own kids. But she's sharp. Used to go to the public meetings.'

'Really.' Test looked at his files again.

'She was close to her mother. Might decide Sean's all her responsibility or she may have had enough.'

'She can't just abandon him.'

George turned to face Test. 'What are we here for ?'

Test reached for some purpose within his files, avoiding George's question. 'I do dislike these changes. Unsettles everything. I had important work at the Centre this afternoon.'

'Oh yeh. And what was that ?'

Footsteps climbed the stairs.

'You wouldn't believe it, George.' Test wiped slivers of sweat from his forehead with a grubby handkerchief.

'No.' George eased back into his chair trying to hide his own nervousness over the imminent meeting. He had met Grigeli before; she was not an easy woman.

'I've got so many things to do...'

'Please come in.' Angel appeared at the doorway. She was followed by Mrs Grigeli. Sean's elder sister had the tired, aggressive face of someone still fighting with her life. Her hair was combed flat, lipstick reluctantly flashing on her lips. She pulled a grey plastic jacket close to her body. It was a cheap coat, bought in the Sunday market and now too small for her. A tangible anger filled the air around her, oozing out from her skin, firing her actions. She had scores to settle.

Angel was careful to keep her distance. 'This is Mr Test, he's the Training Centre Manager.

Test struggled to his feet. 'Pleased to meet you.' He thought about offering his hand, but her thin smile pushed him back to his foxhole behind the filing cabinet.

'And I think you may have met Sean's assessment officer, George Rees.'

George moved forward from his chair but kept a safe distance. 'Hello, Mrs Grigeli, sorry to hear about your mother.' He was aware of the inadequacy of the words, simple meaningless sentiments that meant nothing to him but the world to someone else. A person dies, no one stops.

Grigeli nodded. She was not giving anything away yet.

Angel searched for a position of strength within the room but was forced to remain standing facing Mrs Grigeli. Angel was taller but Grigeli was at least two stone heavier. George retreated to the window, his position throwing him the role of mediator or possibly referee.

'Please take a seat, Mrs Grigeli.'

She consented grudgingly to sit down. Angel took the seat opposite her. She knew she had to run the meeting.

'May I offer the condolences of the whole Team on your mother's death, Mrs Grigeli ?'

Grigeli responded through her eyes. There was a stalled, hanging silence.

'Did the funeral go well ?' Angel was not versed in the easy pleasantries of conversation and Grigeli was in no mood to help her.

'As well as can be expected.'

'Good,' she added with staged sympathy. She was searching for a subtle introduction into the subject of the meeting but could only check her file again. Test dug in further and George waited for developments. Angel stumbled forward. Grasping.

'How is Sean ?'

'You tell me, he's in your hospital.'

'You haven't been to see him then.' She couldn't hide her shock.

'When do you think I've had time.'

'Of course, I was just concerned about about him, that's

all.'

'Well that's a revelation.' She glared at Angel.

'He's okay, I was with him yesterday.' George attempted to cool the fire, his voice light. 'A bit shaken by the routine of the place, but he insisted he's going to turn up for the round tomorrow.'

'Never mind about his round.' Grigeli was seething, any target will do and George had put his hands up.

'It's important to him, he enjoys it.'

'Enjoys it ?'

'And there's the money.'

'He can hardly support himself on that. Fifteen pound a week ?'

'That's all he's allowed to earn or they'll stop his benefit.' He was stung into defence, Sean was too close to him.

'And where would we be without that ?'

'That's not the point. It's a job to him.' George's frustration spilled easily.

'Bloody great job that, delivering papers.' She glared at George, daring him to contradict her.

'Perhaps we can get back to the purpose of the meeting.' Angel managed to slide in her suggestion before George could retaliate. He let the issue go but he knew Grigeli was winning.

'With pleasure. What are you going to do with him ?' She emphasized the words with an anger soaked in years of frustration.

Angel was ready for her but alone. 'Well that presents a difficulty at this present time because,' she paused for emphasis, 'obviously we haven't budgeted for the situation.' She looked to Test for support but his head dipped further into his shoulders.

'And what does that mean ?' Grigeli snapped back, unwilling to be put off by any jargon.

'There is a limit on this year's assessment allocations. We've missed the application date until the new assessment round is due to be re-assessed in the autumn.'

'You haven't got enough money for him.'

Test decided he should make a statement to the meeting. 'It's not that we haven't got any money, it's just that it's all allocated in the wrong places at this present time.'

Grigeli looked for a second at Test then turned to Angel again.

'As I said, you haven't got any money for him.'

'It has to be considered, the various options. I was hoping Mr Dent might have been able to attend.'

'Why ?'

'Sean is still his responsibility.'

'Don't you think my father's done enough ?' She dared anyone to contradict her.

'Well of course, under the present circumstances it would be unreasonable to ask your father to manage alone, but with time and a bit of extra home support ?'

'I can't have him. I've got two kids of my own. Sean's a

lot of work.' She stood on every word.

'I understand that.'

'No, you don't. You can't understand unless you're there.'

'No, of course not.'

'And my Dad hasn't been coping with my mother's illness. He's not at his best right now, and Sean...' She paused, struggling for the right words. 'He sometimes makes it worse.'

'Would it be possible to discuss the problems with your father ?'

'Why ?'

'So we can talk about what he needs in terms of support.'

'My father doesn't want anything.'

'We could increase George's time and perhaps put someone in for a few hours in the mornings.'

Grigeli exploded. Pieces inside of her had been waiting years for a moment to speak. 'A few hours in the mornings ? Have you ever had to look after Sean ? I assure you it's not something that takes up a few hours in the mornings.'

Angel was unnerved but battled on. 'He does attend the Day Centre four days a week.'

'And what's that ? Ten to four and then the bus drops him off and it's so long, see you tomorrow.'

'I still think it is an important service.'

'What the hell does he do at the sodding Day Centre

anyway ?' Her attack lunged towards Test who, despite his dug-out defences, had been ambushed.

'Er, let me see.' He desperately scrambled through his notes. Eventually he located Sean's programme card. 'Sean's involved in a number of activities at the moment. There's the pottery, the dance classes, but they finish in three weeks. He swims twice a week and on Fridays he's involved with George in the skills and integration programme.' He looked up, hoping he has satisfied his inquisitor. Grigeli eyed him disdainfully, relishing the moment.

'Pottery and dance, that's very appropriate that is. It's not exactly useful for him, is it ?'

'We try to offer a broad range of activities...'

'And my fifteen-stone six-foot-two brother's now making flower-pots.'

'Not exactly.'

'Useless.'

'We do try our best with the limited resources available Mrs Grigeli.' He attempted a defence. It was a mistake and he knew it. Grigeli frightened him.

'Limited resources, it's always been the same bloody limited resources.'

'The training centre has...'

'You lot had the same excuse seven years ago. What were you running then ?'

'It had a diffrent name then.'

'That's all you've done.'

'There are a range of aims. We have to develop a general approach to training.'

'Training him for what ? If he's not good enough to do anything then just be honest about it. Let's face it, there's enough useless bastards around. He's got nothing to be ashamed about.'

'There's a work integration programme.'

'A bloody paper round.'

'It's a questions of resources, I feel.'

'Balls to resources. What about the Centre ? You should be ashamed to say you work there.'

Test was but he wouldn't admit it. 'We're not exactly a priority at the moment. The council are very strict on the budget. There's the politics, the...'

'My brother's forgotten out there.'

Test was sinking.

'Mrs Grigeli I can assure you it's not easy to get money out of the council under the present financial circumstances.'

'Sean can't bloody do it, can he ?'

'There are other considerations.'

'What ?' She looked around broadening the challenge. 'Your cosy little jobs ?'

The sentence attacked Test. He breathed out deeply. He'd had enough of this job.

Angel tried to move the meeting forward. 'I do feel we're getting off the point here, Mrs Grigeli.'

'The point.' Grigeli rounded on Angel. 'This is the point.

Sean's life is the point.' A silence sliced the air, shaving splinters that bristled.

George moved away from the window and faced the room. 'Maybe we could find him a place at Andy's house ? He's got a spare room and we could split the bills.'

Angel spun around, snapping at George. 'There's nothing in Andy Day's plan about someone moving in with him.'

'And Bernadette was planned ?'

'That's got nothing to do with it.'

Bernadette Isaacs was moved into Andy's house when her mother died. She was considered safe, middle-aged and didn't say much. The Team thought she was an ideal housemate for Andy. The fact that her family had threatened to leave her on the steps of County Hall if she wasn't found a place had nothing to do with it. It all worked well for a few months. Then the Team finance section began getting large bills for late-night taxis, on account, courtesy of Amber Cabs. Bernadette had found the account reference number and had been seeing the city at night. She also had a fixation about aeroplanes and the airport was fifteen miles away. The Team changed the reference number.

Then Bernadette was found dragging Andy across the floor by his nose. She was trying to help him to the toilet. Bernadette's heart was in the right place. George had liked her. She had the ability to create chaos.

'I think he would enjoy the company.' George offered this slowly. He knew he was outside his authority.

'You're presuming a lot, George.' Angel controlled her anger but it was there, flashing just below the surface.

'Unless you want to ask him yourself there isn't much of an alternative but to try it out is there ?' He was over the edge now. Angel cursed him with her eyes but she was in a corner.

'Who's Andy Day ?'

Angel glanced uneasily at Grigeli before turning to her notes. She was aware of the situation at Andy's house but needed time to think.

'Well ?' Grigeli nudged her.

'Mr Day is one of our other clients.'

'And he has a social services house ?'

'Er, yes, but...'

'And there's room there ?'

'Not necessarily.' She returned to her notes. 'Provisionally there might be some resources for a joint tenancy.' She looked to Test for support but he only shrugged his shoulders. He had no idea of the figures and would be pushed to place Andrew Day from a string of other names he had once heard.

'Is it fully staffed ?' Grigeli used her old knowledge of all the meetings she attended with her mother.

'Mr Day is one of our clients with high support needs.'

'So he has a team of carers.'

'Yes.'

'Could it be expanded for my brother ?'

'Is it possible we might be able to use the underspend money this year ? This will all be provisional, you understand.' Angel didn't like rushed compromises. She tried to keep her promises realistic, short.

'It usually is.'

'And perhaps put a formal bid in next year. If the trial period, and I must stress this, is still working.' She looked over at George, then at Grigeli to emphasize her reluctance. Angel had been criticised by her line-manager over Bernadette, even though it was originally his idea.

George hid a smile. He realised Angel was stronger than she seemed.

'Of course, if it's what your father wants.'

'My father wants out.'

'Do you think your father would benefit from some counselling at this time ?'

'No thank you. We've had enough strangers messing around in our lives.'

'It's a service, Mrs Grigeli. We can't do everything.'

'My mother had to.' Her strength began to crack. 'She loved him but it was a life sentence. I can't. I've got my own life.' Tears coloured her eyes with the voice of her mother.

'I understand the stress.'

'No. No you don't. You just get him a house.' She pushed herself up from the chair, hands smearing tears. 'The commitment was ours, but this is an end to it.'

'It still must be provisional.' Angel stood to face Grigeli.

She stopped and considered her words before replying. 'I'm not sure what you understand about my father but, if you know anything about his problems, you know you can't put Sean back with him.

'We'll still need to discuss changes with your father.'

'He's not interested any more.'

'He must be involved.'

'Why ?'

'He's Sean's father.'

'That's why he drinks.'

'I'm sorry.'

'Don't you dare be sorry. You can't be. Just sort it out.' She held herself close, wanting to forget all this.

'Shall I contact you when we know further details of the arrangements ?'

'How long will it take you ?'

'It's hard to say. Maybe a fortnight. We'll need a few permissions. Will Mr Dent agree to sign the necessary forms ?'

'He'll sign anything you ask him to.'

'Will you be speaking to your father tonight ?'

The questions continued. Grigeli knew she would always be asked questions about Sean. She would always be his sister. She cannot just walk away. The clock on the wall moved on, closer, further away. 'My shift doesn't finish till ten. It'll have to be tomorrow.'

'I need to see him soon.'

'The afternoons are best. He should be there.'

'Yes, of course.'

'I'm already late. Thank you for your time.' She pushed past Angel. She would be docked an hour if she didn't catch the three-thirty bus.

George turned back to the window. They all listened as Grigeli descended the stairs. Angel had words for George as the footsteps receded.

'George, I find it extremely unprofessional to reveal a client's confidential information...'

'Oh, c'mon, we had nowhere to go.'

'It was a totally unrelated case. Andy Day has rights.'

George pulled the collar of his jacket up, ignoring Angel.

'George ?'

'What ?'

'You put the whole service in an untenable position and compromised...'

'How many nights would you like to spend in that hospital ?'

'That's not the issue.'

'I'm sorry, I thought the meeting was about Sean's welfare.'

'That is not a very useful response, it would help if you took some notice of the financial realities.'

'I'm his assessment officer.'

'And I've got thirty other families to think of. I was hoping that, with extra support, Mr Dent could have been persuaded to continue looking after Sean.'

'We always stretch the situation to breaking point, don't we ? Put in the bare minimum to keep the family functioning until it shatters and we have to pick up the pieces.' George walked across the office, daring them to challenge him.

'Very dramatic, George, but useless.' She had heard this speech before. 'Who the hell do you think you are ?'

'I think, the family has gone. You heard her, they've served their sentence. It's time Sean lived on his own.'

'You can't control everyone's life.'

'I'm not trying to control his life.'

'What are you trying to do then ?'Angel moved closer to George.

'Get Sean somewhere to live.'

'You can't even find yourself somewhere decent to live.'

George's eyes narrowed; he was thinking of smiling now. 'Sorry ?'

'Your attitude's always wrong, George.' Angel retreated.

'My life has nothing to do with this meeting.'

'I'm not suggesting...'

George moved closer to Angel. The words were just for her now. 'You should remember your own professional code before criticising me.'

'I'm not sure what you mean, George ?'

'It was good enough for you for one night.' The words stung.

Angel tensed hard, wishing she could strangle George. 'I

will be taking this up with your line-manager in the morning.'

'All of it ?' His smile broke through.

'Fuck you, George.' Angel turned for the door, grasping her files, angry.

'Feel free.'

But Angel was not listening now. George was again too much for her. Test had remained sitting in the corner. He watched Angel leave.

'I'm not sure if I followed that, but...'

'Most of it had nothing to do with you anyway.'

'But I do tend to agree with Miss Angel, that it wasn't necessary to reveal that information to the general meeting.'

George sat in one of the now empty chairs. He pulled out a packet of boiled sweets from his pocket and considered eating one before answering.

'She's married.'

'What's that got to do with it ?'

'Ask her husband.'

'About what ?'

'Anything you want.' George had lost patience with Test.

'I fail to see what her marital status has to do with a client's meeting, George ?'

'So you have an opinion on this ?'

'Of course.'

'And that's it ?'

'I do hope you're not trying to be insulting, George.' Test

was wary. He had been warned about George.

'No, I'm not trying.'

'It's just that with the future of the centre so uncertain, I think it's time we all worked together.'

'For what ?'

'There are certain things we all believe in surely ?'

'What do you believe in ?'

'I'm not sure what you mean, George.'

George slowly put the packet of sweets away. He had had enough of Test. Usually he let Test go, but not this afternoon.

'May I ask how the hell you got your job ?'

Test was thrown by the question. 'It was a long time ago now.'

'Were you always this incompetent or did you have to work at it ?'

'How dare you speak to me like that.'

'They're just words, Test.' He was teasing him now.

'You don't have any respect for anyone.'

'Yes I do. You watch me.'

Test forced himself to his feet. He was going to stand for this. 'You've always been trouble, George. Can't you see there are other people here ?'

'You ?'

Test tried hard to say something to hurt George; his frustration filled his words. 'I'll need to speak to your line-manager in the morning as well, George.'

'Great, you can all have a party in there.'

Test stared at George in disbelief before trembling out of the room.

George returned his gaze to the window and the car-park beyond.

The rain had drifted in across the city, the light drizzling rain of early summer that clung to everything it touched. A hand at the annexe flicked out another cigarette-butt. The firs shivered in a silent conspiracy, shedding needles that stuck to the bonnet of a rusting yellow Horizon.

◆ ◆ ◆

Daikoku

Sean is watching a screen. A screen that flickers out to him, bathing his face in shadows of colour. The screen speaks to him; words, phrases, whole sentences, break away from the moving cars, houses, buses, people that trip across the screen. He begins to understand. The words form in his mind, conjuring more images, dreams, possibilities, opportunities. Ideas of himself, past and present and now the future.

A figure appears, moves forward, fingers touch his shoulder, lightly, gently. A woman's fine hand. She places a cup on the arm of the chair that surrounds him. Then the figure drifts away. He stares into the screen, listening to the words that reach out and touch him, phrases, whole sentences that speak to him. He begins to understand. Watching the images of cars, houses, buses, people. He begins to understand.

◆ ◆ ◆

xi

'Mrs.Evans?'

'Yes, can I help you ?' The tone was brisk but confident. A voice at ease on the telephone.

'George Rees here.'

'Yes ?' There was no recognition.

'Sean's mate from the team ?'

A second of thought, then. 'Oh yes, I'm sorry, I forgot.' Her voice thickened. 'Is there anything wrong ?'

George began cautiously. 'Well, yes and no. I'm not sure if you're aware but Sean's mother's been very ill.'

'Oh I'm sorry to hear that. Is she recovering ?'

'Well no. She died on Monday night.'

There was a dark silence on the far end of the line in Llanishen.

'Mrs Evans ?'

'Yes.'

'Sorry. I thought we'd been cut off.'

'No, I'm still here, Mr Rees.'

'Well I'm ringing up for Sean really. You see, he's been up at the hospital for a few days, but he's hoping Sarah'll make the pictures on Saturday ?'

'The pictures ?'

'Er, yes, I thought you were going to take them in the afternoon, he said.'

'Oh yes, the cinema of course. He said he'll be able to meet us under the clock.'

'He did ?'

'Yes, is that going to be a problem ?'

'No, he'll be there. What time was it ?'

'One.'

'Fine.'

'Will you be there ?'

'Me, er no, but Sean will be.'

'Are you certain, with the bereavement in mind ?'

'No problem, it'll take his mind off it.'

'If you're sure ?'

'Perfectly sure.'

'Well thank you for ringing, Mr Rees. I appreciate it.'

'Don't mention it...'

A succession of harsh staccato pips burst into his ear, covering his final words as the box insisted on more money. He swore to himself.

'Sorry, Mrs Evans I'll have to go. I'm out of change.'

The line was already blank.

xii

'Is it almost one, George ?'

George looked up from his copy of the *Weekend Guardian*. He peered across the square to the clock-tower.

'Another fifteen minutes yet. Can't you read the time ?'

'Course I can read the time, George. Just can't see it all the way over there. It's a long way.'

George took his glasses off and looked over to the clock. It was plain enough to him. He looked closely at Sean. Opticians next week. He would bring it up at the Team meeting. Give Mike something to get worked up about.

The café spilled a few more Saturday-morning shoppers out into the square which was seething with women. Women and bags, men and babies. Kids loose on their own, bored but excited.

A waitress arrived at their table. She picked up Sean's empty cup before moving for George's. His hand appeared over it. He smiled up at her.

'Slow down a bit, love, it's a long afternoon.'

She glared at him, debating if she could ask them to leave. They'd been there almost an hour and this was their only purchase. George raised his eyebrows, inviting her. She scuttled away unnerved by his stare, a deep unsettling stare that she couldn't hold.

'I think I'll go and wait under the clock, just in case I miss them or something.' There was a fire of excitement in his voice.

George ground to the end of the feature he was reading. It was the third time he'd attempted the final paragraph.

'Okay. You've got everything, haven't you ?'

'Yes, George, everything.'

'Money ?'

'Sure, George.'

'Right then, have a good afternoon and don't forget to ask Sarah's Mum if she'll drop you back at the hospital.'

Sean nodded eagerly.

'But if you can't, I'll be in the Park Vaults, right ?' He checked to see if Sean was listening. 'You got the address ?'

Sean pulled a scrap of paper out of his shirt pocket.

'Just show that to anyone if you can't find it.'

Sean nodded keenly again.

'Well go on then, bugger off.'

Sean burst from his seat, knocking into the table behind. A skinny youth spun around aggressively, his face seething with a challenge. He caught George's eye first before turning back to face his own table.

'See you later, Sean.'

'Yeh sure, George.' He ran out of the café, surfing his own enthusiasm to the clock-tower.

George watched him go and waited.

Twenty minutes later a tall, elegant mother holding the hand of a bulging daughter appeared at the tower. Sarah and Sean joined hands. He kissed her shyly on the cheek. Embarrassed, but willing. Mrs Evans pretended not to notice, then began to lead them towards the new multi-screen.

Mrs Evans had thoroughly checked the listings two days earlier and then spent a fraught evening talking to women she knew only vaguely from the club. Women who had daughters the same age as her own. Daughters who had been to the cinema with boyfriends of their own. Girls who had seen the film, alone and unchaperoned. She had settled on a vague adventure movie with a parental guidance certificate. It had been described as exciting but harmless by Evelyn's daughter who'd seemed to guess her concerns. She didn't want Sarah to sit through a kid's cartoon or some stupid story about a dog with a bunch of eleven-year-olds, but the film needed to be sensible.

She walked ahead of the couple holding hands behind her. The queue was mercifully short. The price of the three tickets was a shock but she had insisted on treating them despite Sean's offer to pay. He was a nice boy. She was beginning to like him, a bit clumsy but he looked, well, he looked as if he could be normal.

She pushed two tickets into her daughter's hand.

'You're not coming in, Mam ?' It was a hope and a question.

'No. You'll be fine, won't you ?'

'Yes. But I thought you were going to see the film.'

'No, I'm going to do some shopping. I'll be here when it finishes. You'll wait for me, won't you ?' She pointed at the ticket-booth.

'Yes.' Sarah nodded eagerly.

'Thank you, Mrs Evans.'

She smiled at him. He was a nice boy.

Twenty minutes later Mrs Evans used her own ticket to find a seat high on the right, six rows behind her daughter and Sean.

She was always surprised by the number of single people finding time and comfort in the darkness of a mid-afternoon cinema.

She tried to watch the film but her eyes wandered too easily to the couple below. At first they just held hands. Sarah's head resting on her boyfriend's shoulder. Then later they began to kiss; long lingering kisses during the slower pieces of action. She shifted uncomfortably in her seat. She was sure others were watching. But other couples were kissing too. That's what you did in the cinema on a Saturday afternoon. Pleasurable memories of Richard in The Globe on a Friday night in winter. Huddled together for warmth, his fingers caressing the inside of her thigh. When it rained the roof leaked and the usherette used to move people or position buckets depending on the emergency. She watched the screen while her mind ran old memories. Six months later they were married.

As the film worked itself to its own obvious conclusion she slipped back down the aisle, along the corridor to the ticket-booth.

George was on his ninth beer by the time he guessed Sean must have secured a lift home. He was making promises to people he could never keep unless he spent the rest of his life trying.

xiii

O n a Tuesday morning at Llanishen Leisure Centre the city looks like it is retiring. Grey-haired men and rinsed women wallow back and forth across the sculptured swimming pool. The Age of Capricorn aerobics class wobbles on the first floor bowling green, which waits for the indoor league to begin at eleven. The badminton courts are full with trim if slow-moving pensioners. Pensioners who, ten years before would have been putting their feet up and drinking their way to a well-earned stroke, were now fitness fanatics obsessed with calorie intake and low impact aerobic routines. Addicts to the slow drip-feed of ageing adrenaline that comes with exercise and pain.

Kaite looked out at them.

'God, you didn't get this in Ireland, the old ones know they're past it there.'

She looked at George for a response but he was absorbed in trying to dislodge the brake on Andy's wheelchair.

'When we going to get this thing replaced ?'

'Again ?'

'Yes, again.'

'It's the third in two years.'

'I know but none of them have been any good.'

'Bring it up at the meeting.'

A fresh-faced attendant appeared with a key to the first-aid room. She informed them it was fully equipped with emergency medical kit, oxygen if they needed it and a life-vest.

'God, she was keen.'

'Some are,' chided George.

'Must be new, all the rest look bored as fuck.'

George and Kaite smoothly changed Andy into his swimming costume despite the constraints of the boxed first-aid room. It was a routine they eased into as the murmur of voices and water rippled just beyond the door.

'Now us. I'll wait here with him if you like.'

'I'm not shy if you're not.' She looked at George, daring him.

Getting Andy to the pool was relatively easy as the sides sloped off into a sand coloured concrete beach complete with soft tropical waves that lapsed lazily at the shore. George liked this part of his job. The world was working while he was swimming with a couple of friends.

They attracted a few stares as they stumbled into the

water, but most of the regulars knew them by sight, and once they were covered to shoulder height the odd threesome merged easily with the other swimmers.

'Hey, there's your mate over there, Andy.'

George waved back at a swimmer on the far shore. The old people were easy friends.

George and Kaite talked slowly, savouring the sound of words and voices as the public address played Michael Jackson. Andy's face was washed into bursts of laughter by any wave that climbed over his head. He watched the other swimmers stroke past.

'Look at them all. I'm sure that guy over there was in that stupid film about aliens and eggs in the water.'

A fine-looking pensioner stepped out onto the diving board before tipping off, executing a plausible if rather direct dive.

'You're all heart, Kaite.'

'I know, but what are we doing here ?'

'Community integration.'

'Don't give me that bollocks. That's Angel's fucking cause at every meeting. Integrate fucking everything then normalise it. We're hardly integrated are we ? We've just joined the fucking old folks' home.'

'We're out in the community, a sort of community.' George was smiling. He enjoyed Kaite when she was animated, it gave him a chance to try his own thoughts on a volatile and cynical mind.

'But what does the community think of us ?'

George shrugged his shoulders.

'Like, when I'm up in town, the people, they look at Andy, then quickly at me, then away as if they're ashamed of something. Ashamed that they're glad it's not them, wishing they didn't have to be reminded of it. That we shouldn't be out there disturbing their shopping.'

'C'mon Kaite, last week someone came over for a chat in Sam's. A complete stranger, just said hello, tried to chat, stopped for a couple of minutes then said goodbye naturally. Think how hard that must have been. I can't do that until I'm a couple of pints down.'

'He was probably trying to convert you.'

'We are all part of God's love.'

'You've got to stop going to that church, George.'

'It's part of the community, anyway Andy likes the singing. Don't you, mate ?'

Andy turned with the mention of his name.

'Course you do.'

Kaite brushed Andy's hair away from his face. 'You tell George you want to go down the pub.'

'We go down the pub after. A proper night in the community.'

'But the community, it's, we're not...'

'It's a big thing, the community, we're just a small part of it.'

'That's bullshit, George, you've been on too many fucking courses.'

'Maybe.'

'Couple of weeks back, this man comes up to me on Corporation Road. Sean was pushing Andy, we're just minding our own business and he just says, "Terrible to see them like that", pointing at Andy while handing Sean a quid coin.'

'What you do ?'

'Told him to fuck off before I poked his eyes out.'

'Tactful.'

She smiled. 'I know, but how many others think that ? Sometimes even I think that, that's why I went for the bastard so savagely. Even Arthur,' she waved her hand at someone who was trying to attract their attention from the far side of the pool, 'what's he really thinking ?'

'He's probably thinking when he's going to get a chance to look at you in that black swimming costume again.'

'Be serious, George.'

'I am.'

'George, you're pissing me off.'

'C'mon, it's a Tuesday morning. I'm enjoying myself.'

'Well ?'

'Apart from that, he's just happy enough to take Andy for a swim on his own. Probably thinks he's a friend of sorts. And why not ? I used to have loads of sort of friends.'

'But it's not real, is it ? Not real friends.'

The subtle, absorbed sounds of water and voices surrounded them. Easing.

'Real friends ?' George pondered the idea. 'Real friends are not easy.' He looked at Kaite for a response but she seemed to have withdrawn into herself. She tilted her head back reaching for the patterns in the waves. They pushed gently across the pool, pulling Andy through the water. At the end of the width Kaite turned to George.

'Do you want to go for a swim ?'

'No, I'm fine.'

'I'll go then.'

He watched her lunge backwards into a stroke, eyes fixed on the ceiling. She had a natural grace on the water.

'Well, what do you think of that then ?'

Andy ignored him, still watching the swimmers.

Real friends ? Yes, he had a few real friends, but where were they ? Spike, tall gangly Spike, Private Spike Williams. He hadn't seen Spike for twelve perhaps fifteen years. Some years a Christmas card turned up, some years nothing. Lionel, there was Lionel, always pleased to see him, whenever. Every few months in some pub in town, a big easy smile, curly hair, dark shining eyes. Then he wouldn't see him for another couple of months. Jane, a friend for fifteen years of marriage. Where was Jane now ? London ? Brighton ? Cath in the flat below, sometimes she asked him in for a cup of tea, then asked him to read her mail and pay her bills at the post office if she was too weak to go out. How many friends did she have ? Then the women who occasionally found him attractive enough or perhaps sober enough to invite back. Back to dreary detached semis or one-bedroom flats hidden away off Corporation Road. Women who hoped he would leave early in the morning, as he usually did.

Christ. He shook himself. Sad old bastard. It's not that fucking bad.

He turned around into a faceful of water splashed by Kaite.

'Cheer up, George, pay day Thursday.'

'Aye there's that, Kaite, then the fucking meeting on Friday.'

'How's your scheme to get that lad a room going ?'

'No problem. He'll be living at Andy's by the end of the month.'

'Mike might have a few things to say about that.'

'I've had a quiet word with Mike. He's all for it. Thinks it was his bloody idea. You get no recognition in this game, you know.' He grinned at her.

She splashed water over his face. 'C'mon, you sad old bastard. If you ask nicely you can help me move.'

He looked to see if she was teasing.'You're not moving again ?'

She beamed back at him.

'Where to this time ?'

'I've found this flat, oh you should see it, it's a gem. It's huge, with a kitchen and a living room. And from the bedroom you can even see the castle.'

'When you moving ?'

'Friday afternoon ?'

'Possible.'

'And maybe you can help me warm it up a bit after ?' There is a smile in her eyes, twinkling.

'That would be nice.' His eyes dropped to her breasts which filled out a shiny blue bathing costume. She lifted her eyebrows. There was only one meaning in this. Friday was going to be an interesting evening. 'About four-thirty, ok ?'

'George, you're a sweet.'

She leaned across and kissed him on his cheek.

'Andy, George here is wonderful, you know that ? Wonderful.'

Andy answered with a ripple of laughter which turned into a wave as he threw his head back into the water. George and Kaite joined him as his head resurfaced, spluttering with breath and mirth.

xiv

The words merge together for George. A club, lower East Side. Smoke drifts across the lights at the tables. People do not talk, just sit and listen to the notes from the stage. A car starts in the street outside. The words focus again. More dates and some chord analysis. A waiter clicks two glasses of whisky and rye on the table. The lights flicker. More music and George smiles across to a dark woman at the bar. The back door opens but George misses the sounds. The words have filled his mind again. A scrape of chairs at the bar. Sounds in the kitchen. The music stops to a gentle rise of applause. A kitchen door opens.

'Morning.'

George looked up from the book he'd been reading, unsure of where he was, then he remembered. 'Oh, hello, love.'

'Didn't know Dad was taking in lodgers.'

Grigeli moved away from the kitchen door, across the room to the window. She pulled open the curtains. Light steals away the darkness. George put his book down.

'I just called in.' He stood up, brushing crumbs of biscuit from his jacket. He looked like he had slept in his clothes, which he had. 'Did you get my message ?'

'What?

'I rang your house, spoke to your husband.'

'He was up, was he?' Disdain filled her voice.

'He is now.' George smiles.

'I haven't been home yet.'

'Just finished your shift?'

'Yeh, I usually call in to see Dad. He hasn't been that well.' She remained at the window, looking into the room. George sat down at the battered dining table which filled a corner of the room.

'I don't think he'll be that bright this morning.'

'Drunk?'

'Aye.'

She thought about her father and then dismissed him. 'How did you get in?'

'Philips next door.'

'He rang you, did he?'

'He was worried about Sean when your Dad didn't make it home. It's a sort of standing arrangement I've worked out for a few weeks.'

'Dad didn't tell me about it.'

George shrugged his shoulders.

'Is this the first time?

'Yeh and he's been out a week so that's not too bad going.'

'Is Sean alright?'

'I think he missed his medication.'

'Shit.' Grigeli cursed her father under her breath. 'Dad should not forget about that. He knows he needs it.'

'I found him in front of the tv.'

'He'd had a fit ?'

'I think so.'

'He can't stay here. You've got to get him some care.'

'I'm working on it.'

'"I'll look after him," Dad said. "I'll not have him stay another night in that hospital." How long did that last, aye? Straight down The Langrove for another skinful.'

George flexed his fingers. Nerves. 'We've got a meeting at the house today. It might go through in a week.'

'Should have left him in the hospital.' Grigeli started picking up old newspapers that littered the floor. George would have done this if he'd thought about it but now he just watched. Grigeli was a tired woman, she had watched her mother do this, tidying up after Sean or her father. Now it was going to be her turn.

'He hated it.'

'So what ? Do you think I like working ten-hour shifts while that useless bastard husband of mine can't get off his arse to find a job ?'

George felt her anger, weary. 'I'll get Sean a place in this house. Another week.'

Grigeli pushed the papers and magazines into a rack. 'That woman rang me. Wanted us all to go down and meet Andy what's his bloody name's carers. Told her I couldn't make it because I was working. Suggested I could ask for some time off on compassionate grounds. You can tell she's never worked for Coates Soft Drinks and Orange.' Grigeli smiled at George. 'You know what the perk of my job is ? After a ten-hour shift they give you a carton of juice. Something to take home for the kids. Ask her if she'd work a night-shift for a bloody soft drink.'

George straightened his back against the armchair. 'Angel tries hard. Sometimes she's a bit too focused, if you know what I mean.'

'Is that the same as saying she doesn't live in the real world ?' Grigeli remained in the middle of the room, closer to George.

'No, that's my problem.'

Grigeli pulled away. 'My mother used to think the world of you.' Then she turned to face him, smiling. 'Can't think why ?'

'I have my good points.'

'Well hidden are they ?'

'Underground.'

She watched him closely, taking him in, his short hair, dark grey stubble, broken nose. 'You've been in hospital, haven't you ?'

George stiffened. 'Don't hold back the questions like. Don't spare my feelings.'

'Just something to say.'

'Aye, used to get stitched up after every fight.'

'The type of hospital where they won't let you out.'

'No.'

'Is that why you want to help Sean ?'

'It's nothing to do with that. He just needs a bit of guidance. He's alright, Sean. He's almost there.'

'My mother told me about it. Think that's why she liked you. "A hurt gentleman," she used to say. A hurt, gentle, man.'

'She obviously hadn't seen me box. Pure violence I was.'

'She knew you well enough.'

'Everyone thinks they fucking know me. Couple more conversations and you'll have an opinion.'

'I have that already.' Grigeli moved close to the table, her hands touching the wood.

'Aye, I'm sure.'

'Don't get touchy. Only asking.' She moved away from George. 'Sean up yet ?'

'Sleeping it off.'

'Was he conscious when you found him ?' Her voice had lost its danger for George, but she is only hiding it.

'Out of it. But I think he was sleeping by then. Difficult to wake him when he's like that.'

'Fucking dangerous to wake him.'

'I think he must have smashed the lamp when he fell over.' George pointed to a stand that had supported a white lamp shield.

'Never liked it anyway.'

'He had a couple of scratches on his face.' George pointed to the lower side of his cheek. 'And on his neck.'

'He does that when he's fitting sometimes.' She looked around at the living room. 'How did you get him to bed ?'

'Carried him.'

She looked at George trying to see where his strength was. 'And Dad ?'

'The police carried him.'

'Not again. They charge him ?'

'Apparently not. I think the copper knew him.'

Grigeli smiled. 'Did he have red hair ? Big ?'

'That's the one.'

'Christopher Parry. He used to live at the bottom of the road. Couple of years older than Sean. Liked to think he was his big brother. Chris got into so many fights over him. Stupid things like names, but he wouldn't leave anything go, no matter how big they were.'

George remembered looking up at the policeman as he carried Mr Dent into the house. 'Looked like he could handle himself.'

'He could do that.' A flirtatious smile flicked across Grigeli's face.

'Knew him well then ?'

'Now who's asking the questions ?'

'That's my job. Looking after people, you need to know who they are. Now your father, he could do with some more support.' He put on his fake professional voice for effect.

'What about AA. That would appeal to your little friend at the office.' Grigeli put on what she thought was Angel's voice. 'Would it be possible to discuss the problems with your father ? Talk about what he needs in terms of support ? Do you think your father would benefit from counselling at this time ?' She switched back. 'I'll give her bloody counselling.'

'It's the language that gets you.' George tried to defend Angel.

'It's not the bloody language. It's that she doesn't really care.'

'She does. She just comes across cold. It's the work-load.'

'Slept with her, have you ?'

The directness of the question hit George. 'Fuck mun, it's eight o'clock in the morning.'

'So ?' Grigeli moved closer to George.

'What's it got to do with you ?'

'Thought you had.'

'No.'

'Liar.'

'Why should I ?'

'And I bet she's married.'

'Has anyone ever accused you of being blunt ?'

'Tactful I am. Like my mother.'

'I'd noticed.'

She leaned closer again to George. 'Better than talking about the weather.'

'Yeh.' He began to get up. 'I'll go and get Sean.'

Grigeli stopped him as he tried to stand, then leant down and kissed him. She held it for a couple of seconds and then pulled away.

'What did you do that for ?'

'Wanted to see what you would do.'

'And ?'

'Just as I thought.'

'So ?'

'Nothing.'

George pushed himself up. Grigeli walked away.

'I'll go and check on Sean.'

'Yeh, you'd better do that.'

xv

S ean waited outside Angel's office. He checked his watch. He was sure he was not late. George said that he would be in plenty of time, but that he had to go into the office and wait for Mrs Angel. She would be there at two. The woman at the desk had smiled at him. Mrs Angel was expecting him. He was expected. His cheeks coloured with pride. Someone was expecting him. George was right again.

The woman had led him along the corridor and asked him to wait outside Mrs Angel's door.

'Mrs Angel will be here soon.'

Then he was alone again. He could hear sounds from deeper in the building, conversations, voices. A woman passed him on the corridor. Sean smiled but the thin woman just looked at him. He didn't like that. When people didn't smile at him.

'Hello, Sean.' Angel smiled at him.

'I'm not late, am I ? My father was late this morning. I didn't get ready. I'm not late though.'

'No, Sean.' She checked her watch. 'It's only two o'clock.'

'Cos I wouldn't want to be late. George said I shouldn't

be late for this. I should be on time. That's what he said. I'm always late. I can't seem to help it. I do my...'

'Sean, it's fine. Please sit down.' She led him into her office. There were no papers or files to be seen. Everything had its place. She offered him a chair opposite hers in the middle of the room. A desk was pressed against the far wall, looking out of the window.

'I'm never late for the papers though. George says we're always on time for them. I like that, being on time. When I'm not late.'

Angel waited for him to finish. Sean looked at her, hopeful.

'Has your father told you why you're here, Sean ?'

'Yes.' Sean nodded to help his words.

'What did he say ?'

'That I've got to be here and I've got to answer all the questions.' He nodded his head as if to confirm the instructions to himself.

'And he told you what we will be discussing, talking about ?'

'Oh yeh.'

'And.'

'Questions. I've got to answer them.'

'We're here to talk about where you're going to live.'

'It's okay. I'm back living with my Dad. Not at the hospital. Didn't like it there.' He affirmed this with a desperate enthusiasm.

'I know you didn't enjoy it there, Sean, but it was only a short time, wasn't it ?'

'I like living with my Dad.'

'Your father has probably mentioned the chance of living more independently. Perhaps having your own place ?'

'My Dad says I can always live with him if I want to.'

Sean is emphatic. Angel had not been expecting any resistance. Usually Sean will do anything to please.

She tried again. 'Most people, Sean, when they're older, they have to live alone.'

'My Dad don't want to live alone.'

'Like your sister, she lives alone.'

'She lives with Uncle Michael and my cousins. I'm their Uncle. They call me Uncle Sean.'

'But your sister had to move away. Perhaps not to live on her own but to live with someone else.'

'I don't want to live on my own.' Sean was nervous. He hung onto his thoughts. He wanted to stay with his Dad.

'Perhaps not on your own but with a friend ?'

Sean considered the suggestion. This was possible. 'Like George ? George stayed at our house last night. Perhaps I can live with him ?'

Angel was aware that the interview was slipping away from her. George had not warned her Sean could be like this. But she had to keep going, it had taken three weeks just to set this up. 'Sean, your father thinks you might like to live with a friend.'

'My mother told me I had to look after my Dad. She told me.' He was getting desperate now. Mrs Angel wanted him to move.

'Sometimes the best way of looking after someone is to allow them to live on their own.'

'What ?'

'And the best for you because now you're older you'll have to start doing more things for yourself.'

'I do things for myself, now, honest.'

'There's a young man about your age, needs someone to live with him. He's got a spare room and we thought you might like to meet him.'

'Why would he want me to live with him ?'

'I think he's on his own and you can share the bills and things like that.'

'What's bills ?' He pushed himself back in his chair, away from Angel.

'Money, you need to pay it, for things, to live.'

'I don't pay any money.'

'When people earn money they have to use some of that money to pay for things like water and electricity.'

'I earn money. I spend it at the weekend going to the cinema. I pay for Sarah sometimes.' Sean straightened himself against his chair. He knew about this now.

'Yes, I understand that but now, perhaps, when you're living with someone, sharing a house, you might like to use some of that money to pay for food and things ?'

'Yeh, I might do that. If someone asked me.'

Angel sensed she was at last getting somewhere with Sean. 'This man, his name's Andy. Would you like to meet him ?'

Sean's face fell. 'Does he go to the Centre ?'

'No.'

'Cos I know Andy from the Centre. Don't want to share with him.'

'No, he's not at the Centre.'

'Good.' There was relief in his voice and now Angel's.

'Would you like to meet him ?'

Sean shrugged his shoulders.

'He lives near where you deliver papers.'

'Do I give him a paper ?' His eyes lit up, his voice filled with enthusiasm.

'I'm not sure.'

'Cos if I do I could get him the papers myself. And I wouldn't miss him out. Not when when I knew him.'

'When you meet him perhaps you could ask him.'

'Yeh, I'll do that.'

'So you'll come and meet Andy and think about living with him?' As Sean's eyes filled with panic she realized she had made another mistake.

'I can't leave my Dad. My mother said to look after him.'

'Sean, sometimes, circumstances.' She hammered the word. 'They force people to do things they don't really want to. You'll like living with Andy. It'll be a change for you.

Think of it as a long holiday.'

'I been on holiday. I didn't like it.' He spat the words back.

'Your Dad can visit you.'

'They said that about the hospital.' Sean pushed himself up from his chair. He wanted to leave now. Angel was forced to stand with him. His bulk towered over her. He was nervous and afraid.

'I'm sure he will this time.'

'George said I wouldn't have to go back to the hospital.' Panic began to fill his voice.

'I don't think you will.'

'Cos I didn't like it there. Not a nice place.'

'If you move in with Andy you won't need to go back to the hospital.'

'I don't want to leave my Dad.' His voice climbed, beginning to scream.

'You won't need to leave him alone. You can visit him. On the weekends and things.'

'I see Sarah on Saturdays.'

'You can see your father on a Sunday then.' Angel was as desperate as Sean and losing control.

Sean headed for the door but Angel blocked the route, he turned back into the room. 'I can't leave my Dad. My Mam said.' Sean grasped onto his mother's words, screaming at the room. They will keep him out of the hospital.

'If you don't move in with Andy now, he might find

someone else and you might have to go back to the hospital.'

'I...' Sean turned in confusion. He must get out of the room. She will send him back to the hospital where people scream at you or just laugh and stare. He must get out, he must reach the door. Mrs Angel was trying to send him back to the hospital. He tried to reach the door again but it opened and George was smiling at him.

'Ready ?' George saw the terror on his face. Angel's anger and frustration. They stood in front of Sean, blocking his escape. Sean dipped his head, pushing his hands into his back-pockets. He swayed uneasily, there was nowhere to go.

'Yes, we're ready.' Tension filled Angel's voice.

'I got the car out the back. Down to see Andy, right ?' He spoke directly to Sean, his voice upbeat and enthusiastic.

'Right, George.'

'You'll like Andy. He's a good lad. Lives in this great house where we deliver papers.'

'Really, George ?' Sean's eyes brightened.

'Would I lie to you ?'

'No, of course not, George.'

George smiled at him. 'Good. Go down and open the car, Sean.' He offered Sean his car-keys. Sean took them and moved past George and Angel. His head followed the floor, not daring to look up. As he reached the door George called him back. 'And aye, don't drive it away, right ?'

'I wouldn't do that George.'

'Go on.'

Sean headed for the car park. They listen to his heavy feet running along the corridor, then a door closing.

'How was it going ?' George was cautious.

'I was just explaining the necessity of the move to Sean.'

'How did you do ?'

'Fucking terrible.' They moved back into Angel's room. Neither was ready to join Sean in the car-park yet.

'That good, aye ?'

'I was just about to threaten him with shock treatment.'

'He looked a bit worked up ?'

'His mother made him promise to look after his father.'

'Hell, I was hoping he'd forgotten about that.'

'He's told you about it ?'

'When we first admitted him to the hospital.'

'He'll listen to you ?'

'When I tell him now. But he won't keep listening. I told him about Andy last week, thought it was a great idea, couldn't wait. Asked him about it yesterday, couldn't remember a thing. So I went through it all again. And I mentioned it to him this morning.'

'He seemed keen to meet Andy. When I pressed him on it.'

'I don't know how he'll react. He's not predictable, that's one of his problems.'

'But if it's that or the...'

'Doesn't matter. He might agree to move in. Next week he's back at his Dad's with no memory of living anywhere else.' George slumped into one of the chairs.

'He stayed at the hospital.'

'It was a locked ward. He couldn't get out.'

'Great, George. You came up with the bloody idea.'

'It'll work. Just need to be positive. That's what I need to be.'

'You'll need to be more than that, George. You heard his sister.'

'There wasn't another option.'

'There isn't now.' Angel was sharp with George. She had played along with his schemes and ideas too many times.

'If he likes Andy's and forgets about his bloody mother's promise he might stay.'

'It seemed lodged in there.'

'Sean's memory of what his mother said, maybe we can twist it a bit.' His hand turned in the air.

'You can't do that ?'

'Why not ? What choice do I have ?'

'What happened to your sanctity of self-determination speech ?' There was a certain rancour which cut through her voice.

'Which draft did you read ?'

She turned away from him. 'George, you're a bastard at times.'

'I get by.'

She looked hard at George, then dismissed it. She didn't have time now. 'Have you managed to speak to his father ?'

'Not yet.'

'But you were there last night ?'

'How'd you know that ?'

'Sean told me.'

'Mr Dent wasn't in a very talkative mood.' George rubbed the end of his fingernails.

'Why was that ?'

'Police picked him up outside the snooker club.'

'What for ?'

'Being unconscious.'

'Who told you ?'

'Neighbour rang when he didn't return home.'

'And you've been at his house all night ?' Angel was attacking him but George only teased her.

'Sure, he's got a better tv than me. There was a great film on at four. It was set in New York in the 'fifties. My era.'

'You're getting too involved again.'

'No, I'm not. This is me. I have to live like this.' His eyes challenged her to contradict him. She backed away.

'There is only so much commitment you can give.'

'I've got enough for this one.' He pulled his jacket close. Angel was getting to him.

'What if you leave, George ? What then ?'

'Maybe he'll have enough friends then. A circle, other people to support him. I've read about this system in America. It's really working.'

'That's a different world.'

'And they've tried it in this country. Bristol, I think.'

'It's just another new idea.'

'This one's different. You get people directly involved in his life. Friends who want to be there.'

'You know how hard it is to make friends.'

'This works. We just need to push it along.'

'Who's going to organise it ?'

'It works.'

'We're the only one's who are going to do it, George. And because we're paid for it.'

George stopped himself from replying. He just looked at Angel, drawing her eyes in, then he spoke. 'You're not just in it for the money, Angel.'

'There's only so much. I have my own family. Other things.'

'There you are then.'

'Sorry, I didn't mean it like that.'

'Don't worry about it. I know who I am.'

'Do you, George ?'

George pushed himself up from his chair. It was time to leave now. 'You don't know me, Angel.' He was hiding, running again.

'Don't give me that.'

'Why not ? I'm just the guy in the leather who doesn't give a damn. That's who you want to think George is.' He stood to face her.

'What did I have to do ? Spend six months with you

before I dare say anything ?'

'You only know me through this and one easy night.'

'This is your life.'

'Thanks a lot. I'm that hollow, am I ?'

Angel turned on him. 'You won't let anyone in, will you?'

'I've tried that.'

'And ?'

'Tears and promises.'

'You didn't try that with me. I could have been anyone.'

'Didn't need to.' He pushed for the door again. Angel was too close to him. 'That was me, you just couldn't see it.'

'I'm not who you think.'

'A respectable, married, career woman.' He spat out the words.

'That's right, dismiss it. It never happened. It was just sex.'

'Exactly. You just keep living like this.'

'I will.'

'What do you want me to do ? Say sorry that I only wanted a night with you ?'

George stopped. He looked out, past Angel. Did he care anymore. 'See me Sunday ?'

Angel shook her head.

'Why ?'

'Steve is home this weekend.'

'Next week then ?'

'It's not going to happen, George.' She clasped her files close to her, turning her eyes away. A defence now, it had become too real again. She looked for the door.

George caught his fear as it climbed. 'Na, you're right. It never fucking happened. C'mon, let's get out of here. This place.'

22

i

J oyce cleared the last remaining dishes from the tables. She just needed to wipe the tops down and quickly mop the floor at the entrance to the hall. She would be home by three. There was a game-show on the television with that short little man who used to do comedy.

Sounds of the afternoon drifted through the Centre. Thursday afternoon. Two of the children were talking quietly to each other on one of the far tables. They seemed to be having a romance. They were always together now, shyly holding hands. She had even seen them kiss once, very quickly before the boy caught the bus home. Joyce had cried when she saw the kiss. The other women had asked her what she had been so upset about. 'Nothing. Nothing at all. I just enjoy crying sometimes.' It was lovely to see children happy. She still called them children, even though they were too old for it really. It was easier that way. She couldn't think of them as anything else.

Joyce rinsed the mop into the bucket. She didn't want to miss her programme.

Sean and Sarah didn't notice Joyce. They had lingered after dinner. No one seemed to mind that they were late for the afternoon. It was nicer being together. Just talking. Sean was always talking. Asking questions.

'Is your mother taking us out this weekend ?'

'I think so.'

'Are you sure ?'

Sarah drank the last drop from her cup of tea. 'Yes.'

'Really ?'

'Why ?'

'Because George is away.'

'What's he away for ?'

'Said he was going to London.'

'Why's he going there ?'

'Don't know.' Sean thought hard about this. George going away was still new information for him. 'He goes, then comes back.'

'Perhaps he knows someone ?' Sarah was unconcerned. It was just more words.

'Yeh, that must be it, Sarah. He must know someone.'

'I've been to London.'

'You haven't ?' He didn't believe her. London was beyond anything he could think of as real.

'Yeh, my mother and father used to take me.'

'Really ?'

'Every year. I seen it all. All the sights. The Palace.' She paused, trying to remember images from ten years ago. She could think only of the colours and the rush of people. 'And the other things.'

'My father took me to Newport. That's a long way.'

'Not as far as London.' She was dismissive.

'No, I don't think so. We went on the train though. To see the football.' Sean wanted to compete. London is such a big place, a huge idea, but Sarah had been there. To London.

'My father used to live in London hospital.'

'Why ?'

'I don't know. He used to work there, in the hospital, in London.'

'Does he still live there ?' Sean was unsure now, other memories crowded in. 'He lives in our house, with my mother. Why would he live in the hospital ?' She missed his concern.

'Have you ever been to the hospital ?'

'Of course.'

'What for ?'

'Cos my father works there.'

'I've been to the hospital.'

'My father's hospital ?'

'Don't know, don't know your father.'

'He's tall, he's...'

Sean cut her off. 'Might have seen him.' He didn't want to remember too much about the hospital.

'He knows everyone in the hospital.'

'I didn't like it.' He turned away from Sarah, his face

searching the floor.

'You'll like my father.'

'Why ?'

'Course you will. Everyone likes my father.' She remembered her last visit to her father's hospital. 'People call him sir.'

Sean was not listening. 'Didn't like the hospital.'

'You'll like him. He likes you.' She nudged his arm.

'Does he ?'

'I told him about you. He likes people who got a job.'

'You told him about the papers ?'

'My mother did. She said he likes to know things about people. Who they are. Where they're from and things.'

'Did he know people in London ?'

'Course he did. He knew everyone there.'

'Imagine knowing everyone. That would be great.'

'Why ?'

'Er, I could go and see them.'

'You couldn't go to London.'

'I could. I could if I wanted.'

'How ?'

'I could catch a train, or bus or something. I could catch a bus from the gardens. I always catch a bus from the gardens.' He pointed away, to the gardens, to London.

'Not to London.'

'And I could pay with money from the papers. I could pay with that. Then I could. On the bus.' He smiled at Sarah, he had worked out a way to go to London.

'If you did that, where would I go on Saturday ?'

'I'm not going this Saturday. And if I did I'd take you with me.'

'You'd take me ?'

'Sure I'd take you. We could go with George. He wouldn't mind.'

'Yeh, ask George.'

'I bet George knows everyone in London as well.'

'My mother wouldn't mind then. She likes George.'

'Does she ?'

Sarah thought hard over the answer. She was keen to get the words exactly as she had heard them. 'She says he's reliable. That's what she said.'

'I'll ask him tonight after the papers.'

'Where would she stay ?' Sarah was thinking back, remembering when she was a girl in London.

'We'd come back with George.'

'We couldn't do that. You always stay in London.'

'I couldn't stay there. I'm living at Andy's.'

'You don't stay at Andy's every night.'

'I do. I pay Andy money, for my room. And we share everything else.'

'You stayed at your father's last Saturday.'

'That's different. I'm allowed to stay at Dad's. That's what my mother said.'

'I bet George stays in London.' Sarah was becoming

impatient with him. There are always problems for Sean.

'No he doesn't. He comes back.'

'Not the same day.'

'How would you know ?'

'We always stayed in a hotel.'

Sean turned away. Sarah was always disagreeing with him. He didn't want to be told he was wrong all the time.

She nudged his arm. 'Would you like to stay with me in a hotel ?'

'And George ?'

'No, just us. Me and you ? We could stay together ?' She looked up at him, smiling.

'What about George ?'

'You don't want George with you all the time do you ?'

'Of course not.'

'When he takes us to the lakes. You wouldn't want him with us all day, would you ? Watching ?' She was testing him.

'No way.'

'We could have a room and a bed together.'

'In London ?'

'My mother and father always had a room on their own.'

'Really ?'

'The hotel was big, and there were hundreds of rooms. And maids and lifts and things.' Her hands climbed in the air in an effort to paint pictures of the magical hotel she remembered.

'We could have a room.'

'It'd cost money.'

'I got money. I got thirty pounds. My Dad keeps it for me.'

'That'll be enough.'

'I got more than that.'

'You'll ask George then ?'

'Yeh, no problem.'

'You are working tonight ?' This was her idea now. She needed to make it work. She knew George. He'd make it happen.

'Yeh, I'm working. People like to get their papers on a Thursday.'

'You ask him. We can go then.'

'It'd be good that.'

'You won't forget ?'

'No. I'll ask him after, in the park.' George was his mate. He'd take them to London.

'Good.' She smiled, leaned over and kissed him. Then, breaking away, she headed for the door. Sean caught her before she could leave. He kissed her at the entrance to the dining hall.

She tried to pull away, laughing. 'I got to go now. Mrs Wilson's class.'

'I know.' He kissed her again. Longer. She finally pulled away, blowing him a kiss as she began to run along the corridor.

Sean turned to see if anyone had been watching, but Joyce had finished clearing and was sitting in the kitchen with enough time for a cup of tea before catching the bus home.

ii

Merches Gardens was full of Summer and children. They had been abandoned for six weeks of bored freedom and the Parky was tired of chasing them off the flowerbeds. P.C.Davies was tired of phonecalls from the Parky about "wanton vandalism". They were bound to wreck something so it might as well be the flowerbeds. At least you could plant them again next year. P.C.Davies hadn't discussed his new approach to community policing with the Parky but then he wasn't up to belting around town trying to catch kids who were much faster and fitter than he was.

'Aye mister, give us a paper.'

A short freckled kid with a tap for a nose looked up fiercely at George.

'Do you want a broken nose kid ?'

The boy's eyes opened wide in amazement that switched to fear as George widened his own and stared. The boy turned and fled to the safety of numbers under a big oak tree in the far corner. George chuckled to himself. He didn't like being disturbed when reading the paper. He brushed through the final pages pausing only at the For Sale ads. They were usually more interesting than the news items. The things people tried to sell. Sometimes he would ring a number for some obscure item and get an in-depth description of its unique selling points. He loved listening to people describe something lovingly that they wanted to get rid of for fifteen quid.

He was intrigued by the prospect of seventeen pounds for an adapted ironing board when his partner in papers loped up and sat on the bench.

Sean smiled confidently straight ahead, waiting for George to open the conversation. Time passed. He began to shuffle as George moved onto the sports page but the eagerness to talk pushed him forward.

'I've finished George.'

'Ave you ? How many you got left ?'

'None George.'

'None ?'

'I delivered them all.'

'Good.'

George dipped back into his paper.

'And the ones I didn't deliver I put in the bin by the chip-shop.' George turned to him but Sean continued quickly. 'You do that, don't you George ?'

'I know that but... It's just that..' he struggled with an explanation.

'That's okay in it ?'

George decided trying talk it through was hopeless. 'Never mind, you've delivered them now.'

A ripple of reserved applause drifted over from the bowls

green. The summer championship was progressing as slowly as the season.

'What you think an adapted ironing board looks like Sean ?'

Sean looked at him unsurely before shrugging his shoulders.

'No, me neither.'

Sean shuffled on the seat, waiting to find his own words.

'Big meeting Thursday, George.' There was a nervous edge to his voice that he tried to disguise with an enthusiasm gleaned from Mike.

'Aye, big meeting. You all set for it ?'

'Think so.'

'How do you think you're getting on ?'

Sean didn't reply immediately. His face was absorbed in a determined sobriety as he tried to measure the correct response.

'I like it, George. It's nice there. I've got a room of my own. Andy and Mike and Kaite, they're good, George. And the others. I like it at Andy's, it's nice.'

'You just tell them that and everything will be fine. They all like you.'

'They do, George ?' There was a bright hopeful surprise in his voice.

'Yeh, sure they do. They enjoy having you there, especially Andy.'

'Really ?'

'Of course they do. It livens things up.' He winked at Sean who smiled shyly back, scuffing his shoes on the concrete to hide his embarrassment.

'How long is it now ?

'Three months.'

'Goes quick, don't it ?'

'I put posters up this week.'

'Yeh ?'

'My father gave them to me.'

'Aye.'

'He came around to see me he did. On his own.'

'Good.'

'I won't have to go back to the hospital now, will I ?'

'I shouldn't think so.'

'I don't want to go back there again. Not unless I have to. I didn't like it there. Not,' he stuttered. 'Not a nice place.'

'It'll be fine as long as you keep looking after Andy.' George was confident that the initial trial period would be continued. His own report, which the Team had expected to be unreservedly glowing, had appeared with a measured tone that accepted the problems but effectively dismissed them as adjustments. Even Angel had been impressed. There was a psychologist's report plus an assessment by an occupational therapist who owed him a favour to back it up. Sean was staying.

But in truth it really was going well. Andrew's behaviour hadn't changed at all. He seemed to accept Sean as another of the many people who constantly moved in and out of his life. Whether he realised Sean was there for the duration was anyone's guess.

'I will, George. Me and Andy are mates.'

'That's good, he's a nice lad.'

'Why can't he speak, George ?'

'It's just one of those things. Some people just can't.'

'He's older than me.'

'Aye, a few years.'

'He had a birthday party last week. That's when my Dad came to see me. Kaite was there. And Mrs Angel came.'

'Houseful.'

'Why didn't you come, George ?'

George turned his face to the sky. 'Couldn't make it Wednesday.'

'Andy had a cake with candles.'

'How old was he ?'

'Thirty-four, George.'

'You had a good time then.'

'Andy enjoyed it. He smiles all the time, so I know he likes me.'

'He's happy, I guess.'

'That's what it must be, cos he's always smiling.' Sean thought back to the birthday party, full of people. They had even sung a song. He liked singing. They always sang at the football matches. The new season would be starting soon, so his father had said. He could go to the football again. His father always took him to the football matches on a Saturday. And when they got home there would be egg and chips on the table. Unless they stopped in Caroline Street for pies. He liked that. Caroline Street pie and chips. They'd always get an extra one to take home though. 'Andrew hasn't got a mother either, has he, George ?'

'No, not any more.'

'I wish my Mum didn't have to go away though, George.'

'I know you do, Sean.' He hesitated, knowing he'd been over this ground before. 'Things just happen sometimes. Can't do anything about them.'

Sean straightened himself on the bench, eyes looking straight out. 'Dad says she's in heaven now and if I'm good I can join her one day. That's right, init George ?'

George dropped his head, following the easy movements of his own hands as he folded the paper away. 'It might be.' His words were slow, unsure of themselves and their meaning. 'But you'll be good anyway, won't you ?'

'Yes, George, course I will.'

'But not too good, aye.' He nudged him with an elbow, smiling weakly.

'No not too good,' replied Sean with a seriousness that forced a laugh from George. But Sean was not laughing, he was considering his thoughts.

'Where's heaven, George ?'

George realised he had to answer. 'I don't know.' He

hesitated, hating his reply as he ducked out. 'But I'm sure your mother will be happy there.'

This seemed to placate Sean momentarily, but he was determined to continue.

'I wish she didn't have to go there though, George. Dad says I can't visit her or anything, not like when she was in hospital. I could visit her then.' His head fell, unable to go any further. George allowed the park to absorb the silence. There was no answer to any of this.

More bowls were rolled across manicured grass, a clash of wood on polished wood. A pair of woodpigeons clattered into the high branches of the full chestnut behind the bench. Conkers were beginning to swell at its fringes and some leaves were already beginning to colour. The tree was protecting itself for the assaults of the autumn.

'How's Sarah ?' George attempted a cheerful tone to lift the gloom. Sean immediately brightened.

'She's great, George. Her mother's taking us to the pictures again this weekend.'

'Hey that's great. What are you going to see ?' He was relieved to be off the subject of death.

'I don't know. Her mother usually picks one for us.'

'I'm sure you'll enjoy it.'

'Yes I will. It's dark and we can kiss in the cinema,' he added wickedly, eyes sparkling with fun.

'Don't you watch the film ?'

'Yeh, George we do, but Sarah likes kissing.'

George nodded. What else were the pictures for ?

'Sarah likes kissing, George.'

'I'm sure she does.'

'I like kissing, George.'

'It's good fun, most people like kissing.' A cautious edge seeped into George's answers.

'We do other things as well, George.'

'In the cinema ?'

'No. Not there, George.'

'What do you do, Sean ?' He asked him carefully, unsure which way to go.

'You know, kiss and...' He clasped his hands between his knees.

George waited. 'Yeh, and ?'

'And kiss.' Sean turned away from George. 'I don't know.'

George relaxed. 'You and Sarah, you happy, Sean ?'

'Yeh. She likes kissing, George.'

'Good. Any problems, anything bothering you, ask me, right ?' George began to fold the remaining papers in his bag. The bin waited for its weekly delivery.

'You know when you go to London ? Do you stay there?'

'Yeh, of course.'

'All night ?'

'Aye.'

'Why do you do that ?'

'Friends. I stay with friends.'

'Could we come with you ? Me and Sarah ?'

'Why would you want to come with me ?' George stopped folding the papers. 'Don't you see enough of me in the week ?'

'Course we do, George. But we could stay in a hotel with a bed.'

'I don't stay in an hotel. I couldn't afford it.'

'I can, George. I got money.'

'You don't stay in a hotel. It's too expensive.'

'Me and Sarah will.'

'There's plenty to do here without going to London.'

'Don't you want us to come with you ?' Sean hadn't been expecting George to say no. George always said yes when you asked him.

'It's not that.'

'I want to stay in a hotel with a bed.' He had promised Sarah.

'Perhaps you can come with me later in the year. A day-trip or something.'

Sean dipped his head down. 'Sex is good, isn't it, George?'

George looked out into the park. Why this afternoon ? 'Yes, it's good, with the right person.' He looked down at his shoes. 'Well, it's pretty good with anyone really.'

'What do you mean, George ?'

'Nothing Sean. It's just sex, it needs to be with someone

special, someone you know very well.'

'I know her very well.' His face reflected his belief.

'Yeh, course you do, but...'

'You wouldn't do it with someone you didn't know well, would you, George ?'

George clenched his fist. 'It just needs to be special, that's all.'

'It is, George.'

'Course it is.' He was thinking hard, trying to think what to think, what questions to ask. 'Look, have you got, you know condoms and all that ?'

'Course I have. Don't be daft. Condoms.' Sean swept his hand away dismissively. 'Sorted all that, no problem.'

George tried to study Sean's face, but was conscious they were both uneasy with the subject. How much did he know? How much had they done ? 'You haven't told anyone else about this, have you, Sean ?

'No way, George. I wouldn't tell anyone else.'

'Well, promise you won't tell anyone yet, especially her mother, alright ?'

'Don't be stupid, George. I wouldn't do that.'

'Good, course you wouldn't, right. What the hell am I on about, right ? You're a working man.'

'What do you mean, George ?'

'Nothing, mate.'

They slipped into silence as a man pushing a Tesco trolley stopped on the path in front of the bench. He looked carefully at the bin, examining it from a distance without considering Sean or George. George watched him as he moved closer to his quarry before dipping his hand quickly into its wire mouth. With the flourish of a magician he spirited three cans, brightly coloured but battered and empty. He seemed to study them carefully as if there was a regulation size limit for empty cans before tossing one back while retreating with the remaining two to his trolley. He dropped his catch deftly into a black bag before pushing the trolley onto his next waiting pot.

'C'mon, let's get going then or Andy'll be thinking we've deserted him.'

They eased themselves up from the bench. George folded his remaining papers for the waiting bin which bulged with crisp packets, kebab wrappers and one steel coke can.

'Old Collins never could count.'

'Never could, George.'

'Seeing Sarah tomorrow ?'

'I see her almost every day now, George. Sometimes I see her in the evenings if her mother's got enough time.'

♦ ♦ ♦

Benten

Sean is watching a screen. The screen speaks to him, words, phrases, whole sentences break their way from the moving cars, houses, buses, people that trip across the screen. He begins to understand. The words form in his mind conjuring more images, dreams, possibilities, opportunities, the future, his future. Ideas of himself past, present and in the future.

A figure appears, it moves forward, standing behind him. A hand touches his shoulder. Lightly, gently. A woman's fine hand. She places a mug on the arm of the settee that envelops him. Then the figure drifts away. Sean smiles easily to himself. He stares into the screen, listening to the words that reach out and touch him. Phrases, whole sentences, that speak to him. He begins to understand. Watching the images of cars, houses, buses, people. He begins to understand.

♦ ♦ ♦

iii

'If we can all read the minutes of our last meeting.' Angel's voice was bright and confident. In control. She was at her best in meetings, possessing a sharp, frightening efficiency that intimidated the unprepared.

George stared at his photocopied sheet. Meetings were a boring but necessary chore that he endured once a month. He liked their air of incipient democracy but despaired at their endless prevarication on decisions. There was always a need to consult a physio, the finance officer, team policy or Andy's long-departed sister who stared down from the gruesome reality of her short-lived marriage on the wall. Kaite had once suggested a woman called Marilyn who could read auras. George thought she was being sarcastic but the meeting took her seriously and promised to consult Team policy on the reading of auras.

The minutes of the last meeting summarised new rota arrangements, Sean's continued tenancy, shopping days at Sainsbury's now changed to a Thursday and the possibility of using Andy's mobility allowance to lease a car. Mike had researched the leasing of a vehicle for Andy with an obsession bordering on dementia, and now proposed a metallic red Montego complete with an adapted front seat and three-year warranty. He had stressed the last item as if the first thing the new Montego was going to do when released from the showroom was break down.

The decision to consult the physiotherapist was noted.

'All agree with the minutes of the 29th of July ?'

There was a murmuring of assent among the crowd packed into Andy's living room. George shared the settee with Kaite and Sean. Mike helped Andy drink another cup of tea. Angel chaired the meeting from a perch near the door. A thin, wizened woman occupied the remaining armchair. George had seen her skulking around the Team headquarters but still hadn't worked out what she did. He was looking forward to finding out what exactly the Team paid her fifteen thousand a year for.

'Can I recap on the new rota changes. I believe they're working out ?'

There was another general nod of assent but George could see Mike gathering his dispersed mind to say something.

'Yes ?'

George and Kaite settled back into the settee and waited. George thought he could hear a whispered prayer from Kaite but it could have been a blasphemy.

'Well, it's just that on a Sunday night the wife visits her mother's and she doesn't get back until eight o'clock.' He looked directly at Angel, waiting for a response but still appeared surprised when it arrived.

'So ?'

'I have to get in by six, don't I, and that leaves the boys on their own for two and a half, possibly three hours.'

'And ?'

'Well, before, I could get in at eight and they'd only be on their own for half an hour at the most, but now it's two and half maybe three hours. Any other day and it's fine, but the wife has got to visit her mother on a Sunday because her mother's getting bad and she can't get out as much as she used to and up in Tonyrefail the buses, the buses...'

Kaite spluttered a laugh into her tea which she attempted to stifle with a rasping cough, her face colouring with suppressed mirth. Mike stalled, allowing Angel to wrest the initiative back. He had a tendency to go on.

'Yes, I can see the point, but it's only once a month you'll be working on a Sunday night. Can't your wife rearrange her Sunday visit ?'

Mike stared at Angel as if she were suggesting a family murder. 'Miss her Sunday visit ? The wife's been visiting her mother every Sunday since we were married. It's important to her, the one day out a week.'

'If I was her I'd be out every fucking night,' Kaite whispered to George.

'Well,' Angel stalled, unsure where to go.

'I thought your boys were in comp ?' George decided it was time to join the fun if only to wind Kaite up.

'Shut the fuck up, George,' Kaite hissed at him from the

depths of the settee.

'They are.'

'How old are they then ?' asked Angel.

'Well, Simon's nearly thirteen and Peter fifteen. They're doing really well, Simon's...'

'Yes, well, don't you think they might be old enough to look after themselves for a few hours ?'

'On their own ? On a Sunday night ?'

'Yes, you know, watch the television or something. Simon's nearly sixteen, after all.'

'Peter's nearly sixteen, Simon's only twelve.'

'Yes, well, you know what I mean.'

'I'm not sure. The boys and I have been together on a Sunday night since they were born.'

'God fucking help them.'

'What was that, Kaite ?'

'Nothing.'

'I'll have to discuss it with the wife, and I know she's not going to be too happy either way.' He folded his arms across his chest with studied defiance.

'I bet she fucking won't. Might mean another hour of him.'

Andy moaned for another drink of tea, covering Kaite's whisper. George swallowed a custard cream and passed one to Sean who shrugged his shoulders.

'I'll note that you're going to consult your wife on the problem and we'll discuss it next month.'

'What about next Sunday ? I'm nights then.'

There was a silence as she studied the rota.

'Yes,' she added, unsure of her next move and willing Mike to be as co-operative as Andy.

'I'll stay on an extra two hours if you like.' Kaite smiled up at Angel while trying not to laugh as George nudged her.

'Will you ? Thank you Kaite,' gushed Angel as if Kaite had just volunteered to solve the Irish problem. 'Is that alright, Mike ?'

He nodded reluctantly, still unsettled by the suggestion he had to consult his wife.

'Well now, that's resolved, can we move on to the next item ?' Again she looked at Mike. Why this meeting ? she thought to herself. 'The physiotherapist's report on the car.'

Mike leaned forward, firmly settling himself to absorb every syllable of the next three spoken pages.

Angel read the report in a low monotone. As she summarised the conclusion she sensed Mike's angry frustration. When she looked up, he lunged out.

'That's ridiculous, the advantages of a car far outweigh the negative, and what was that bloody rubbish about the possibility of an accident ?'

'It's got to be considered.'

'Everyone buys a car, but they don't worry about flying through the windscreen when they're driving out of the showroom, do they ? "Sir, this is a lovely car but have you thought about the possibility of compound skull fracture ?"

Like hell they say that.'

'I'm sorry but the OT feels that any accident would seriously injure Andy's legs, resulting in compound fractures.'

Andy turned to Angel at the mention of his name. He had a broad grin smeared across his face which threatened to break into a giggle.

'So, because of this remote possibility that we might have a crash - and I haven't had a crash in twenty-three years of driving - Andy can't have a car to get around like every other bugger.'

'I didn't write this report,' Angel added defensively.

'Do we have to listen to it ?'

'I'm afraid so.'

'It's like the business with the light bulbs.'

'Oh, don't bring that up again.'

Kaite giggled quietly to herself as George nudged her. The great light bulb issue had flickered on for three months when a relief-worker in another area had electrocuted himself while changing one. The Team policy had been hurriedly changed to require 'all maintenance, removal and replacement of electrical appliances to be undertaken by a qualified County electrician'. The call-out fees were huge and doubled over the weekends when the policy extended itself to call-outs only in an absolute emergency. Most people ignored it but the policy was there and Mike had argued with it for three months as if it were a personal attack on his abilities as a handyman. The Team now knew that Mike had renewed the electricity supply to the whole of St. John's Terrace during the heavy snowfall of January, 1982.

'It's just the same bureaucracy gone mad and we just accept it all.' He looked around for support. Everyone dropped their heads except for Sean who smiled blankly at him.

'Well, if you feel strongly on it I can only suggest you write to the Team leader requesting a review.'

'And the trains, you've got to ring up in advance now if you've got a wheelchair so they can put a ramp on for you. I mean a crash, compound fractures, so what ? It's not as if he's using them, is it ?'

'Mike ?' Angel's question forced him to apologise.

'Sorry, Andy.'

Andy laughed but Mike was still simmering. The Team leader would be getting another letter from his regular correspondent.

'Item three, holiday proposals. George, I believe you were going to carry out some research on this ?' She looked up expectantly.

A warm surge of tension slithered over George as he tried to remember when he had agreed to the task.

'Next month.'

'Next month what ?'

'It's a bit early to go booking autumn breaks yet.'

Angel eyed him suspiciously but relented.

Mike pulled a piece of paper from his wallet and waved

it at the meeting. 'I've had an idea on that one. I cut it from the Sunday supplement.'

Angel turned reluctantly to Mike and his piece of paper.

'Boating holiday on the Broads.'

Kaite stifled another giggle.

'The Norfolk Broads ?'

Mike nodded. 'Lovely place.'

'Yes, I'm sure it is, but is it suitable for Andy and his wheelchair ?'

'There's a company that specialises in adapted barges. Electric lifts with routes planned so you can get on and off at suitable points and see the sights.' Mike bubbled with renewed enthusiasm.

'Sounds good,' added George.

'Yes it does. Can we have some prices and dates by next month then, Mike ?'

'Certainly.'

'How do you fancy that then, Andy ?'

The room looked for an answer but he only smiled, abstractedly, as if aware they wanted something from him but was unsure what.

'Can we move on now to number four ?'

Five heads conscientiously looked down to scan the agenda.

'Slippage account.'

Angel stirred her black coffee before daring to explain the intricacies of the slippage account.

'It appears, due to underspend in this year's budget, the Team has a surplus of around nine thousand.' She proceeded carefully, the meeting was only half-interested and that half was interested in the money. 'And we've been asked whether we can think of anything to spend it on.'

'A new car,' offered Mike.

'A new sofa,' suggested Kaite.

'Yes, that's a good idea, Kaite. It's getting a bit worn around the edges.'

'What do we need a new settee for ?'

Angel looked bemused with George's question.

'I don't think it's a question of absolute need.'

'Why not ?'

'I think it's more a question of financial realities.'

'Realities ?'

'There's money available.'

Yes, but do we want it ?'

'It was only a suggestion, George.' Kaite folded her arms.

'I'm not sure what you mean.' Angel was prepared to be patient.

'What's wrong with this one ? It's not as if Andy uses it much. Can't we throw it at the holiday ?'

'No, it has to be a capital purchase.'

'A new wheelchair then ? I was only saying a few weeks ago that Andy's is crap.'

'Sorry, that money has to come from a diffrent fund.'

'But there's no money in that fund.'

'Not at the moment.'

'Hell mun, just give it back then.'

'We can't do that, it'll disappear.'

'So why don't we just say we don't need it now and carry it over into next year ?'

'But we do.'

'No, we don't.'

'George.' Angel lowered her voice as if in preparation for a long monologue to an errant child. 'If it's not used this year it will go back into the central budget and we'll never see it again. Furthermore, if we don't spend it all they'll consider we don't need as much in our budget next year and cut it accordingly.' She looked at him as if the simplest economics were going to be beyond his ken.

'So if we do well this year and actually save money, next year we're going to have to save the same again.'

'Precisely, plus inflation.'

'So everyone's spending this money even though they don't really want it ?'

'Yes, George, but you see, they need it.' She looked around for support but the rest of the room was thoroughly bored. The thin, wizened woman had glazed over and didn't look as if she was in any need to contribute to the general ramblings of the room.

'I'll recommend a settee then. Next item. Sean's tenancy.' She smiled sweetly at Sean who beamed back as he always did. 'Sean ?'

iv

The room is dry, full of the warm smells of drying clay. Dust drifts in the air and lays a thin veneer on all the flat wooden surfaces of benches and chairs which fill the room. Long narrow windows look out over fields of allotments to the marshes. The marshes stretch down to the Channel and the muddy brown sea beyond. Cars blur, rush on in many colours on the road which curves to the lower side of the city. No one is watching.

Sean and Sarah kiss like the lovers they have become. Tender, warm kisses that pull them together when they are alone. It is hard to be alone but terrible when they are not.

Sean touches her, warm, easy, wet fingers. This is not the first time. The first time was at the lake in the deep shade of a sycamore tree. Very quickly. Very hard. No one sure what they were really doing. Now it is longer, more urgent, softer.

Sarah feels him as he pushes her against the bench, moving her legs apart. Wanting every part of this. He is not shy now. This is sex. This is what you are supposed to do.

She does not hear the door of the room open. Sean feels nothing but the excitement of making love to his girlfriend.

A hand grasps him roughly on his shoulder.

◆ ◆ ◆

Bishamon

Sean is watching a screen. The screen cackles and splutters through the static but there is no sound, merely light touching Sean and the faded brown armchair which surrounds him. Lines trammel through the light; reaching out as if to cut but his face remains pale. A peel of laughter cuts in from the street. A splash of light then nothing.

Sean stares into a screen of shadows in black and white.

◆ ◆ ◆

v

Test flicked through the timetable; not reading it. Not seeing anything but a pale young man, frightened and angry, lashing out.

He raised his eyes to the window, another lorry rumbled past, out of the industrial estate on its way to the by-pass and the motorway. Out of the city, past the converted airforce camp, converted again and again until it was allowed to decay into an Adult Training Centre. Another lorry forgotten as it headed east.

A fly, weak with dust and the frustrated hope of glass, stirred on the sill, its legs and wings moved briefly before it gave up, exhausted. Then silence, except for the gentle clock on the whitened plasterboard walls. Test moved across to the windowsill, he looked down at the insect, then moved back to the desk, 'Fucking place,' he thought, 'it's had enough of me.'

He flicked a cuff-link; hoping it would all go away. Leave him alone in his carefully constructed eyrie, away from the bureaucracy that frustrated, the meetings where managers scored points and mined the foundations of sand. Here he was safe. Mr Test to the adults, to the officers just Test, the Mr slipping easily from his name.

Then George stood rigid before him, hands splayed on the desk, spelling out his words, a question, what happened, what happened here, tell me, words struggling with anger, and he knew he must answer.

'Sean has absconded.'

'Yeh, they told me that in the message. Any particular reason ?

'It's a bit delicate, George.'

'Delicate ?'

He paused, breathing deeply. 'We've had a bit of an unfortunate incident.'

'Concerning Sean ?'

'And Sarah Evans.'

'Are they okay ?'

'Yes fine, we think. At least Sarah is. She's at home. As I said, we can't find Sean.'

George stepped back from the desk. 'I thought he'd finished with that. What the fuck happened ?'

'Calm down, George.'

'You tell me what happened then.'

Test took a deep breath. 'You're aware that Sean Dent and Sarah Evans have been having what may be tacitly termed a relationship ?' He chose his words carefully, drawing them out.

George nodded. 'I've been taking them out on the odd weekend.'

'Yes well, the relationship has developed.' He hesitated, searching for the right words. 'Developed further than we anticipated.'

'What do you mean ?' George stressed his words taut, 'Further than you anticipated ?'

'I was under the impression that it was to be conducted on a purely platonic level.'

'And who gave you that assurance ?' His question was sharp and threatening and Test wanted to back his words away.

'You did.'

'Rubbish.'

'You implied it.'

'You took what you wanted.'

They glared at each other. Test dipped his eyes. He knew

he didn't possess the anger to confront George.

'Anyway, that's irrelevant now. They have evidently developed a close personal relationship.' He hoped the words would temper George's anger; he was aware of a long reputation.

'Yes, I was aware of that. So ?' He dared him to argue.

'You knew that and you didn't inform us ?'

'What the hell has it got to do with you ?'

'I am responsible for Sean Dent's and Sarah Evans' personal safety.'

'Not their bloody sex-life.'

'They're not supposed to have a sex-life.'

'Says who ?'

'Sarah's mother for one.'

'Fuck, you haven't told her ?'

'It was my obligation.'

'Bollocks.'

'For Christ sake, George, she's not even sterilised.'

'You bastard.' His anger forced him to spin away from the desk in frustration. Away from seizing Test, shaking him, forcing him to realize.

'I find your attitude very unhelpful, George. I would have expected more support from you in this delicate situation.'

'Support ? I expect Sean and Sarah could have done with some support. If not discretion, but no, they get you exposing them like some fucking journalist.' He talked away to the wall, to himself.

'For your information, they were exposed, as you put it, by Mr Watts in the pottery room and he's made an official complaint.'

'An official complaint? What the fuck for ? I suppose they messed up his precious clay ?'

'Apparently Sean struck him.' There was regret in his voice but George didn't hear it.

'What would you do if Watts pulled you off the top of your Missus on a Saturday night ?'

'Judith has nothing to do with this.'

'And neither has bloody Watts.' But his anger had gone. He dropped his voice as if addressing himself. 'A bit of life, that's all he wanted. He was hanging onto it.'

Time, thick with thought, edged on; the clock, ticking out of time, waited.

'I'm afraid we are going to have to suspend Sean for a week.'

'Don't tell me, unsuitable behaviour.'

'Will you be able to explain the situation to him ?'

'If I can find him.'

'It'll only be for a week or so, George. Just for appearances. The other clients.'

'Unsuitable behaviour. Where else are they supposed to do it ? '

'It's not as simple as that.'

'He hasn't got a car or a place of his own, where are they

supposed to do it ?' He spoke to himself, tied down with a tight control.

'According to Mrs Evans they're not supposed to do it at all.'

'Oh, for fuck sake mun, you ever tried stopping ?' He smiled at Test.

'George, I sympathise with what you're trying to do for Sean, but you must appreciate the situation. The realities.'

'Sure I do.' George turned his head out to the light, the realities turning within his mind. The realities he could do nothing about. Sure.

'He's an adult but he's not in control.'

'He hasn't got rights. Go on, tell me.'

'You know the situation as well as I do, George. It's not so easy any more.'

'It's never going to be easy.'

'When I first joined the service...'

'Don't give me that. I've heard it before.'

Test got up from his desk and walked towards George. 'You don't listen to anyone else. Unless it's in a book you're not interested.'

'Yes I do. I listen to Sean.'

'And where's that got you ? Did you think this out ?'

'I was getting there.'

'And how long would that have taken you ?'

'Easy for you to say. What the hell have you been doing for the last twenty years ? Look at the fucking place.' He raised his hands to indicate the shabby walls and broken plasterboards on the ceiling. 'It's falling down.'

'It's been my life too, George.'

'And you settled for it.'

'I knew what I could do.'

'So you haven't risked anything, have you ?'

'No. I've stayed together.' Test threw this at George as they shouted at each other. Test had read reports on George, reports about the hospital.

George stepped closer to Test. 'Leave me out of it.'

'You need to hold back.'

George pulled away from Test. He didn't want to argue any more. 'He was doing alright for himself.'

Test returned to the edge of his desk. 'Maybe you'll be able to talk to Sarah's mother ?'

'Yeh, maybe.' George thought over the problems, the mistakes he had made. He was annoyed that he had let it get this far. 'You've no idea where he ran to ?'

'He was heading into town.'

'Great.'

'Watts couldn't hold him. Apparently he was shouting something about going to London. Does that mean anything to you ?'

George smiled, at least he knew where Sean was. 'He'll be at the Gardens.'

'What'll he be doing there ?'

'He'll be waiting to catch a bus to London.'

Test looked puzzled. 'You can't catch a bus from there to London. They go from the station.'

George stared at Test, not sure what he could say.

Test looked back. 'What ?'

'Never mind.' He began to dismiss it all. Time to move on. 'And Sarah's okay ?'

'Her mother picked her up.'

'Right, I'll get down to the Gardens.'

'Shall I contact his father ?'

'Not worth it. Unless you want to ring round a few pubs.'

'Not really, George.'

'Where's Watts ?'

'Gone home sick.'

'Lucky, that.'

'There's no need for that George.'

'There was no need of any of it.'

George left. He'd catch the next bus to the Gardens. He might even arrive before Sean.

Test stood alone in the office. There was nowhere to go.

vi

A young woman stares into the mirror and herself. Tears streak her face. Dried out and bitter like anger. She lifts a tube of lipstick carefully to her mouth. She holds it in front of her face, her hand steady.

There are footsteps on the stairs that lead to the bedroom. Her mother's footsteps, but she does not hear them. They are rushing to her.

Sarah's hand flashes across her face. She screams at the red marks which appear with each short pull of her hand.

Her mother runs across the room. Stumbling over strewn clothes and broken glasses, pieces of jewelry. The uniform of the game.

Sarah shouts, trying to pull away, but her mother holds her close as the pain sears through her.

'It's alright. You haven't done anything wrong.' She strokes her daughter's hair as Sarah cries into her chest. 'It's alright, don't worry. I'll speak to Dad.'

It ebbs away.

They are silent, holding each other in tears. The pain waits. It will come again but not as hard.

vii

The rain, sketching, breathed patterns of wind over the rippled veneer of the pond. George watched. A young girl appeared, sixteen at the most. He ordered another coffee, white no sugar. A machine whirred life into the café. Another sketch, this time on the window, pressing. She was late.

The pond was recovering from a long, dry summer. The water was grey and filled with clouds. The Autumn rains had pushed the edges out but not high enough to cover a thick ring of mud which still fringed the shore as if someone had let the plug out of a dirty bath and forgot to scrub the sides.

A child threw stale bread at the ducks on the water. The child was not big enough to throw the bread over the mud and the ducks reluctantly waddled across the shore to his offering. His eyes turned bemused to his father. It was not the same, feeding ducks on the mud.

'Sorry I'm late.'

George stood to greet her. She was taller than he remembered, somehow older, but the lines mapped a fine woman.

'Just here myself.' He offered his hand which she shook politely.

'Coffee ?'

'Yes, yes, please.' She sounded tired, not at ease, hoping this was not going to be as difficult as she feared.

George called the waitress and ordered another coffee.

'I'm just glad you agreed to come.'

She looked at him, surprise seeping through before she recovered.

'Yes, well, I thought it best.'

'Thanks all the same.'

He stirred his coffee. The waitress arrived with a second cup.

'Sarah ?'

'With Richard.'

He nodded. He wasn't sure what he had to say to her. He had thought of something conciliatory, reassuring, but now as he looked at her, obviously composed, dealing with it as she had probably had to deal with a score of crises. Other traumas he knew nothing about. What could he say ?

'She's not too upset ?'

'It was a very traumatic experience for her.'

'Of course.'

'She's upset. But perhaps she'll be alright. She's quite a practical girl despite everything.'

He couldn't quite follow her meaning. Nor think where to begin. 'Yes, very confident when we're out, more than Sean even, almost er...'

'Normal ?' She cut across him.

'Not what I was going to say but...' He stopped, again unsure. 'Sorry.'

'It's okay, that's what I think. A few more seconds of air and it would have been alright. I wouldn't need to deal with any of this. It would be just the easy things.'

'You can't think like that.'

'Why not ? You do anyway.'

'She seems a happy girl.'

'We do our best, Mr Rees.'

George hunched himself down into his jacket. 'I'm not doing this very well. I just thought I should speak to you, explain things.'

'How are you going to do that ?'

'Try anyway.' He thought about more words but they danced away from him.

'I suppose you think I'm old-fashioned, interfering, Mr Rees ?' Her eyes were deepened to sadness by her own guesses.

'No, not at all,' he lied.

'No matter. I should have been expecting it really. She's old enough easily, but she's still young.'

'Perhaps they all seem young to us.'

'Yes, maybe. Perhaps she would have seemed young however old she was, but...' She paused briefly, losing her words before collecting her thoughts again. 'But I have to make that decision for her now. She doesn't see all the possibilities as I'm sure you're aware.'

'Sean asked about condoms, he knows enough that way.'

'So you knew about it ?' The actual subject they were edging around appeared as the unwelcome guest at the tea-party.

George retreated. 'He mentioned something, but it's hard to know how much...'

'And you think he knows enough ?'

'I was working my way through it.'

'And how long would that have taken you ?' She pressed George.

'He only just mentioned...'

'They've been seeing each other four months.'

'Yes, but he...'

'Something could have easily gone wrong ?'

'I know that but they had...'

'Do you, Mr Rees ? Do you really know what could have gone wrong ?'

'It's always a risk, whoever you are.'

'But you weren't at risk.'

George felt the words bite into him. 'No.'

'You don't see it, do you ?'

'Yes I do. I just can't think of them as anything but two young people.' He pushed himself back from the table.

'I don't think Sean was taking advantage of her, Mr Rees.'

'He wasn't, I'm sure.'

'You were supposed to be taking them to London.' The words accused him.

'I never said that. Sean asked but I couldn't have done that.' George looked away. An elderly couple left the café.

'Not without speaking to me ?'

'It was just one of his ideas.'

Mrs Evans looked out across the water. 'Sarah asked me about London too. So maybe I didn't want to listen to what she was saying either.'

'I was listening. I always listen to people.' George spoke inward, to himself.

'You don't understand. I want her to enjoy herself. It's just I haven't had a chance to explain it all. There's so much to it. Sarah can have her life, it's only...' She paused, looking for the right word. 'Natural.' She looked out through the window. The wind flirted with the surface of the water. 'Although I'm going to have a hell of a time explaining that to Richard. He doesn't really want her to grow up.'

'But she has.'

'He won't see it that way.'

'He's a doctor.'

'So what ?'

'I just thought he would have seen other things, other people.' George moved his hands, trying to explain other people to himself.

'Yes, of course he has, but this isn't other people.'

'No.'

'It's not Richard I'm worried about. If she gets pregnant, what then ? Who's going to bring up the child ? Me again ? I couldn't, not again, and Sarah, she's not up to that. She's capable, but not for that.'

'She'd get support. Care homes ?'

'You can't believe that ?'

'Sometimes.'

'I know you've got Sean's best interests at heart and probably Sarah's but you only work with him. You're a friend, we're family. Friends lose touch. But we can't, we've always got to be there.'

'They could move in together somewhere. Get a council house, share a life. I've been reading about it. It could work.' His enthusiasm flared again.

'They're children underneath, Mr Rees.'

'No they're not, they can't be. They're different, that's all.'

'Is that what you really think ?'

'They could live together.'

She stared hard at George. 'Why are you so involved ?'

George looked down at the table. 'He's my friend. I have to be.'

'What else ?'

George raised his head to hold her gaze. 'Nothing, it's just me.'

She looked at him sadly. 'Yes, perhaps you're right.' She paused, unsure of herself for the first time. 'You're a romantic like that, aren't you ?'

'It's happened before. I've read about it. I'll convince

them.'

'That's not so easy, convincing people.'

'I'm good at it.'

Mrs Evans looked away. She understood how George's commitment scared people. They just couldn't believe he was that much involved. It was never just work for him. The realities used to scare her, but not any more. She turned her thoughts back to the future. 'The council hope we'll take care of her, then when we die they'll pick up the remainder and you know what ? They're right, we'll probably do that.' She retreated into her own thoughts.

'With a house maybe they'll be okay. There'll be other people around, help them make decisions.'

'Would you like that ? Someone making your life, not family but half-friends, employees.'

George allowed his mask to slip. 'Dunno. Maybe I could use more support.'

'You're not married, Mr Rees ?'

He shook his head. 'Not any more.'

'I'm sorry.'

'Don't be, she's better off without me. I drift.' He paused, his words sticking. 'And when I don't drift, I drink, not a happy combination.'

'No, I guess not.'

She leaned across the table to hold his hands. He was breathing heavily, deliberately, controlling his thoughts.

'They'll be alright, Mr Rees. I can cope with it.'

Clear tears bathed the corners of his steel-grey eyes. Too much, she thought. Too much thought.

viii

A ngel stirred in the bed, her eyes half-open to the glimmer of the street lights. She was not sure why she was awake. There was no sound in the house. An empty silence covered everything in the darkness of the early morning. She caught the rush of a car on the tarmac in the street beyond, heading back into the city. Her eyes began to close, then a harsh rapping sound pulled her completely out of sleep.

She drew the sheets back and picked up a dressing-gown from a chair at the side of her bed. The polished floorboards were cold. Hard, bare wood that creaked as she found her way across the landing.

The rap from the door came again as she descended the stairs. She pulled the dressing-gown closer. It was three o'clock in the morning. She knew who was at the door. A shiver of excitement or cold caught her as her foot found the colder tiles of the hallway and she saw a figure silhouetted in the porch.

George was about to knock the door again when Angel lifted the latch and pulled it away from him. He walked past her into the hallway. She shut the door behind him. Angel had been wondering when he would come. It should have been months ago. He turned to meet her. Moving close, he kissed her once on the cheek, then quickly on her lips. Angel pushed him gently away.

'It's late.'

He smiled back. 'Yeh, couldn't make it any earlier.'

She led him into her living room, touching a light in the corner which glowed up from the floor. George looked around at the wealth. The order of the house. A piano sat silent in the corner. He wanted to live in a house like this.

'You shouldn't have come here.'

'I was passing, thought I'd call in.' He touched a few notes from the piano. The late and dark music that he loved.

'At three o'clock in the morning ?'

'I always walk at this hour, clears the mind.'

'What if Steve was here ?'

George continued playing. 'He's not.'

'You didn't know that.'

'I checked with his firm.'

'You ...' Angel turned away. Wide white blinds blocked out the street beyond. George was someone she could love or hate. 'I've told you it's not going to happen between us.'

'And I'm saying it is.' He stopped playing and replaced the lid on the piano.

'I'm married, George.'

'You don't love him.'

'That's none of your business.'

'There's not many chances at this, Angel.'

'You don't understand, me do you ? I don't want your life.'

'Are you going to leave him ?'

Angel looked away. 'Yes.'

'Come with me.'

'Where ? To that tiny little flat ?'

George sat back on the piano stool. 'I've told you before, leave my flat out of it.'

Angel laughed. She had always laughed with George. The dark laughs that no one else but George could see. 'I couldn't live with you. I've just realised I can't live with Steve.'

'I'm leaving it, Angel, come with me.' George knitted his fingers together.

'No.'

'Out of this city.'

'What are you going to do ?'

'I don't know yet. Sell flowers ? People must be happy when they buy flowers.'

'For funerals ?'

He closed his hands. 'I've thought about that. I'll have a street-stall. You don't buy funeral flowers from the street.' He was talking to himself now.

'Where are you going to go ?'

'Back to London.'

'You hated it.'

'It had its good parts.'

'Not where you'll be living.'

'I'll get a better flat, housing association, somewhere down in Battersea, close to the market. We'd be alright there. Sean and Sarah can come and visit. They can have a room with a bed. Yeh, that's the answer.'

'You're not blaming yourself for that ?'

'Course I am. I should have listened to him.'

Angel moved slowly in the arc of the room, circling George, keeping her distance. 'I heard Mrs Evans was more reasonable than you expected ?'

George smiled. 'Bloody *Guardian* reader. I had her down as a reactionary. More real than the lot of us. She'll be taking them both to sex education classes next.'

'You are too close to him.'

George turned his head to the floor. 'Yeh, maybe.'

A brown tabby cat twisted its body around Angel's legs. Her hand fell to stroke its back. 'It's late, George.'

'And ?' He stood up.

'You've got to go.'

'No I haven't.' George walked towards Angel. She remained standing. Her head turned away, her eyes on the picture of a naked woman which hung on the wall. The woman leaned over a wash-basin on a stone floor. There was a window in the picture which looked out on a meadow in France. It was summer.

'It was one of those things. It just happened.'

'I know that, I just want more.' He touched her arms

with his open fingers. Her head shook slowly, still looking away.

'There isn't any more.'

'Tonight ? I'm going then.' His hand moved down and touched her bare leg. His fingers slowly moved up to the soft skin of her thigh. She raised her head to kiss him.

ix

The jazz club is as full as it ever gets on a Saturday night, which is not full. Twelve regulars, seven of them alcoholics, are strewn with the chairs. A stage, one step above the level of the masses, hides away in the furthest, darkest corner. The corner seems to draw in the smoke from the rest of the club, pulling a thick veil that the regulars insist improves the rhythms and adds to the ragged edge that all the musicians seem to cultivate.

George was not a regular but regular enough for the doorman to allow him two concessions. He had found a table close to the stage but near enough to the bar. He could never fully convince himself he liked jazz. But the club had an air, a promise of lost conversations, theories and ideas that would change the world. Aimless thought. Thought that seeped through the boards, staining the ceilings with nicotine and sweat. The music ? The music was for the dark corner, a background to thinking.

He'd never taken Sean to the club before, but tonight was short notice. He needed to get out and George could only think of the club. Sean looked content enough, a bit morose, but so did the regulars. He watched the bubbles rise from the side of his glass of bitter. Sounds were fluid through the smoke, muffled, half-spoken words, the scrape of a chair across the wooden floor, cash register opening then closing. Rise of louder, livelier voices from below.

'You wanted to come out tonight, didn't you ?'

Sean's eyes remained fixed on the rise of the bubbles as he answered. 'Yes, George.'

George's own thoughts were still filtered with words from Sean's mother. Tired and wise. 'It's better to get out, see. The music will take your mind off things.' A voice from a year back when they used to go the rock nights at the Royal Oak. He leaned closer to Sean in order to emphasise his words. 'It's over now, try to forget about it.'

Sean remained staring at the beer.

'Is this a pub, George ?'

'Yeh, sort of pub, club.'

'Are they going to play music here, George ?'

'Course they are.'

'Not many people in here though, George ?'

'It'll fill up. There's a good night in here, you'll enjoy it.'

Sean looked around the bar. 'Not many people in here though.'

George took a slow drink from his bitter before replying. 'But we're here. Me and you.'

'Usually go to the cinema on a Saturday.'

'Yeh, I know that but...'

'Sarah's mum picks the film for us. I pay though, George. I got money. Do you want a drink, George ?'

'I'm fine with this one for now, Sean.' George touched the top of his full beer glass.

Sean returned to staring at his beer. He was struggling with events, trying to sort them in his own mind. His actions, the frustration of not being able to control his feelings, future. 'We didn't do anything wrong did we, George ?'

'No.'

'Sarah still goes to the Centre, don't she ? Every day. Then on the weekend we go out. Next weekend, George ?'

'We'll have to see how things work out.'

'You said it was good, didn't you, George, and everybody does it, don't they ?' He was certain of this in his own mind but wanted his friend to confirm it.

'Some people don't like to be reminded of it, that's all.'

'I'll be able to see Sarah again, won't I ?'

George hesitated before answering. 'Sure, you'll be back at the Centre in a week.'

'But will I be able to take her out next weekend ?'

'We'll have to see what her mother says. You know she's not happy with you at the moment.'

Sean smiled to cover his embarrassment. George tried to banish his own grin but failed. This bolstered Sean's confidence. He sat straight in his chair, pulling his shoulders back. He was thinking and with a great effort of concentration asserted his mind.

'Sarah's alright though, George ?'

'Yeh, don't worry, she's fine.'

'I want to be able to see her, George. I don't want it to be like Mam, I don't want her to go to heaven.'

'It's not like that. It's just that you've split up for a while, that's all. Lots of people split up.'

'I don't want to split up though, George.'

'I know that, sometimes it just happens, that's all.' He was addressing himself, searching for distraction as he scanned the room. 'Here we are, mun,' he indicated the man who had stepped onto the stage. Sean followed his gaze. There was a burst of clapping following his appearance which Sean chorused enthusiastically. The guitarist barely acknowledged the reception before he embarked on a tortuous tuning of his instrument. Two men joined the audience, settling at the table nearest Sean.

'What's he going to play, George ?' The customary enthusiasm had returned to Sean's voice.

'He's going to be playing some jazz.'

Sean tried to absorb this information before furthering another question.

'What's jazz, George ?'

'It's...' He stopped himself as he considered the question, unsure how to answer it. Usually he just sat and thought about everything bar the music. Sean peered at him expectantly.

'Well, he sort of gets up there and plays what he wants to think, he sort of follows the rhythms.'

'Will he be like the Stones, George ?'

'Not exactly like the Stones. I don't think he'll be singing.'

Sean seemed satisfied with this for an instant but then continued, intent on a story.

'I like the Stones, George. My Dad used to buy me all the records. I used to have a record every Christmas. Do you think he'll get me one this Christmas, George ?'

George was distracted as he clawed for an answer. 'He might. No I'm sure he will. What's the latest album ?'

Sean shrugged his shoulders. 'I don't know George.'

'Never mind, they're all the same, aye.' His eyes sparkled but Sean just looked at him blankly.

'He bought me a poster.'

'Have a drink, Sean. Got to keep quiet when he's playing.'

Sean nodded, took a quick drink and then continued speaking. 'He always gets me the latest album. I used to like The Police as well, but you can't get them any more, can you, George ?'

'Er no, they split up.'

'Like me and Sarah ?' His eyes lit, clutching at a common reference.

'A bit like that.' George hunched down into his jacket, trying not to notice the other regulars, two of whom had turned around to see who was talking.

Sean appeared satisfied by this answer and turned his attention to the guitarist who had been playing a long, involved introduction. The music stuttered out and Sean returned to the conversation. One of the men who had taken up the table next to Sean turned to see who was talking.

'Why isn't he going to sing then, George ?' His voice hadn't adjusted to the hushed concentration that had descended over the room.

George, conscious that they shouldn't be talking, lowered his voice. 'They don't in jazz.'

'I like singing, George.' He concentrated briefly but his eyes widened in amazement as watched the musician perform.'Why is he closing his eyes, George ?'

'I'm not sure, we'll talk about it later.'

'Sure George, we'll talk about it later. I couldn't play with my eyes closed though. I wouldn't be able to see. I can play you know, George.'

George bowed his head uneasily, hoping Sean would run out of things to say. The man on the table next to Sean who had turned a couple of minutes earlier turned again, this time more aggressively, and directed his speech sharply at Sean.

'Look, mate, I didn't pay two-fifty to hear you ramble about your fucking guitar playing.' He glanced at Sean then turned to face the stage again.

'Why did he say that ?'

'Ignore him, Sean.'

'But I was only talking.'

The man leaned over again, this time directing his question to George. 'Can't you shut him up ?'

'No.'

The man stood up and took a couple of steps closer to George. 'Dunno why you bring people like that in here.' He pointed at Sean.

'Like what ?'

'Like him.'

'That so ? And you're an expert.'

'I'm trying to listen to this music.'

George stared at the man, holding his gaze. He was sure he'd seen him around. Not in the club but somewhere else. 'Why don't you try an' do that then ?'

The man turned his face away from George. 'You think you'd have some consideration for others.'

Sean spun to George, there was a desperate incomprehension in his eyes. George put a finger to his lips trying to calm him. The guitarist spun to a final chord which broke into a ripple of hands, allowing George to suggest that they should head out to the back of the club and the stairway down.

'Why did he say that, George ?' Sean stood on the landing of the stairway. His hands were shaking, tears welled in his eyes.

'Some people are just like that Sean.'

'But George, I was only talking.'

'I know. He held Sean's shoulder. 'Don't worry about it, not everyone is like that.'

'But George, I...'

'Look, Sean, I want you to do me a favour, right ?' He peered closely at Sean, insisting he return the stare. 'Here's a five-pound note. You go out on the street and get a taxi home. I'll catch another one in a while.' He looked at him carefully to see if he was following his instructions. 'Can you do that for me ?'

'I don't want to go home yet, George.'

'I know that, but we have to. I'll write the address down just in case you forget it, right ?' He fished in his jacket for a pen and tore a beer-mat along its seam to uncover a clear piece of paper. 'Just give this to the taxi driver and he'll get you home. Tell Kaite I had to stay out, alright ?'

Sean reluctantly took the butchered beer mat but was still unsure.

'Are you clear what you're going to do ?'

'I'm enjoying myself really, George. Don't send me home like my Dad. I don't want to go yet.'

'I just need you to do this for me. Okay ?'

He nodded once.

'There'll be plenty of taxis, you just catch one home.'

Sean nodded again. George thought about more words but decided he could add no more. He tried to touch Sean's arm as he walked away but he shrugged him off.

In the club the guitarist was rambling through another solo. George walked over to the bar where he checked his pockets for change under the light. He picked out three coins which he held firmly in his right hand. His eyes found the two men sitting on the table. They were deep in a whispered conversation and did not see George as he strode over to their table. The doorman had noticed him return but just watched from his stool at the door. The man who had spoken to Sean looked up as George dumped three coins into a pint glass, half-full of beer, on the table.

'Here's your fucking two-fifty mate.'

The beer spilled over the glass and onto the table. The man stood up sharply, straight into the knuckle-filled hand of a left uppercut that sent him sprawling across the table. His friend was slower but George wasn't and another arm fired out, connecting sharply. The two men struggled with the flatness of the floor as the doorman tackled George from behind.

Light and noise, as his face skidded into the wooden floor. People scattered, the music stopped and he felt the sharp hard blows of fist slam into his temple.

He thinks he can see a man on the stage, illuminated by a single beam of light. He mouths unconnected words. This kind of life. Swallowed truths, unintentioned lies. Barren rooms, intended friends. I search in static, soul-less screens. Search for a picture never clear. A cameo.

x

Another voice, clear now. Brutally clear, issuing instructions.

'I will count to three and you will rise to your feet, is that understood ?'

George nodded his head.

'Is that understood ?'

'Yes.'

'Right, one, two, three, up.'

George straightened his legs with the lift from his captor. He could feel his arms twist behind his back as they were locked back and the sharp cold pinch of metal burn against his wrists.

The lights were on in the club and a blur of faces rushed past as he was forced towards the door.

'Fucking wanker...'

'He just bloody hit them, no reason...'

'42 Tewkesbury Road.'

'Where are they ?'

Then the steps clattering up to meet him as he slipped from the first landing. The first big hit and a scuffle into the corner.

'Are you pissed ?'

'Uh.'

'He's not coherent, his legs went.'

'Be a bit more careful next time, Canton. We don't want to lose him.'

More stairs.

'Keep your legs up.'

Faces at another doorway. People stared at the captive. Part of the entertainment. His legs slipped away from him again.

'Walk straight, you bastard.'

Night. Orange sodium and flashing blue bathing the white of a van. The turn of a handle, doors opening.

'Feet up. Come on step in.'

The dark, welcoming interior away from the lights and the noise of street and doors shutting firm behind. He stumbled as the van pulled away, falling again into the darkness which pulled him down and surrounded him.

♦ ♦ ♦

'Fuck, he's been sick.'

Two white faces peered into the back. George was sitting on the far side of the van, huddled into the corner.

'Come on, out you come.'

He tried to focus, his eyes searching the faces.

'Are you alright ?'

'Yeh, just getting my vision.'

♦ ♦ ♦

'Name.'

'George Rees.'

'Date of birth.'

'Sixth of the eighth, forty-nine.'

'Address.'

'189 Cathedral Road.'

'Is that a flat ?'

'Flat 5.'

The details droned on. The simple facts of his life and identity put brutally on paper. A single man nudging fifty living alone in a bedsit in a tired old city. His thoughts came back to him, removing the blurring and leaving a thudding pain that stretched across his skull.

'Do you think you could remove these handcuffs ?'

'No way. We had information that you were being extremely violent.'

George looked at the desk sergeant. Lines scoured his face, hidden only at the edges by a dark beard that was turning to grey. He was a man who had seen a lot of rubbish in the city. The darker side that people tried to ignore in the pale light of a winter's day.

'The arresting officer has had information that you were violent. Are you intent on continuing this behaviour ?'

'No sir.'

The sergeant smiled grimly through his beard.

'Release him.'

'But sarge ?'

'Release him. He's not going anywhere.'

The young PC walked behind him.

'Lean over the desk.'

George pushed himself over the desk, his head touching the duty record which was still blurred in his vision. The steel tightened further, his teeth clasped together in the sharp rush of pain before relief.

'Thank you, sir.'

'Can we continue now ?'

'Certainly, sir.'

The details continued. Information he didn't need.

The doors of the cell closed around him. He hadn't been inside one since the army. They hadn't bothered to take his boots away from him then. A pale green light filtered through from the duty room where he could hear more voices arguing. It was useless to argue once you were inside. No one was going to listen to you yet. A malefic odour of detergent and dried urine hung as if as much part of the regulation as the green paint on the walls and single washable bed. He felt a surge of vomit and looked quickly for the source of the smell. A walled-off cubicle that held a steel-rimmed bowl caught most of what he had left inside.

He wiped a stream of saliva from the side of his mouth, then felt carefully around the side of his head, massaging the bumps slowly. Someone had caught him from behind. He felt a trickle of blood slip down from his forehead. A deep cut pulsed with warm blood, that smeared his fingers. He'd had worse, but not for a few years.

He edged back to the bed as his eyes adjusted to the gloom at the edges of his vision. He sat back, hard against the wall. Above the door in scrawled brown letters was the legend *Grabham was here*. He found himself wondering where Grabham was now.

The door moved open and a shaft of light followed by the cell lights pulled him from a shallow sleep.

A PC he vaguely remembered stood in the doorway.

'Rees, are you awake ?'

'I am now.'

'Get up, your solicitor is here. Mr Shannon.'

The PC was replaced by a thin man in a dark coat. His eyes looked as if he had recently been dragged from sleep or at least a good restaurant. They were eyes much older than the face that held them. A face that had only just passed youth but the eyes seemed out of time.

George blinked up at him before pushing himself off the

bed and offering his hand.

'Good evening. George Rees. Sorry to drag you out.'

'That's fine, Mr Rees. It's what I'm paid for.'

The door was pulled behind them. A faint click as the metal locked.

'Are you feeling ok ?'

'Yeh, sure.'

'The blood ?'

'Just a bang on the head. I'm fine now.'

'The arresting officer wants you detained until the morning when you're sober enough to make a statement, but the desk sergeant thinks you might be able to give one now.'

George's shoulders sunk as he sighed with the weight of the evening.'What do you think ?'

'I think you should try and make a statement now. If this goes to court it'll look better that you were lucid enough to answer questions.'

'I'm fine. The slurring's due to the bump on my head. Not used to it any more.'

'I'm sorry ?'

'Used to box. Badly.'

'Right, well we won't need to mention that. I'll just get the interview arranged.'

He pushed himself back up from the bed and tapped on the door. It opened immediately.

'Just get me out of here.'

'I will, Mr Rees.'

Canton and a second officer led George back through the chargeroom to a small, well-lit room beyond. His solicitor followed.

'Will you sit there, please.'

The formality of the setting surprised him and for a brief, pure second he was grateful to be living in a democracy. Canton shuffled his papers and set himself in a chair opposite George. His training officer at Cwmbran was still shouting at him but he was going to get this one right.

'Are you ready to be interviewed ?'

George nodded. Canton leaned forward to a box on the wall and inserted a black cassette. He looked up to Mr Shannon, who nodded. He pressed a button and began speaking.

'This interview is being tape-recorded. I am PC 1070 Canton. The time by my watch is 23.09. The date is Saturday the 17th of October 1996 and the interview is being conducted in the interview room at Cardiff Central Police Station. I am interviewing. Can you give me your full name and date of birth please ?'

'George Rees, sixth of the eighth, forty nine.

'Also present is,'

'PC 7084 Andrews.

'And,'

'Mr Shannon.'

'George, can you confirm other than those persons who identified themselves there are no other persons present in this room ?'

'I can confirm that.'

'Prior to departure you will be given form number F325. This form will explain your access to these tapes.'

'Which form is that ?'

'This form. The form that I will give you at the end of the interview. Do you understand ?'

'Yes.'

Canton droned on through the legal advice that George was entitled to, ending with the warning that he no longer had the right to remain silent. He remembered signing some petition against it in the city centre one Saturday afternoon. He could remember signing a sheaf of petitions. His scrawled signature stacked up behind a line of other names all protesting against Indonesia in East Timor or vivisection or the dockers' strike, things over which he had no control but he always signed. Time passed. His concentration drifted back to Canton who had remembered his lines well.

'...remind that you do not have to say anything but it may harm your defence if you do not mention something now and rely on it later in court. Do you understand that paragraph and what it means ?'

'I understand that paragraph, yes sir.'

'The purpose of this interview is that I will be putting a

series of questions to you and I will give enough time to answer my questions. Do you understand that ?'

'I understand that, sir.'

'Before we start, the purpose of this interview is for you to give an explanation of what happened at an incident earlier on this evening. What I'll be doing is, I'll be putting a series of questions to you and I'll be giving you time in which to answer my questions. At certain periods of the interview I may or may not introduce a special warning in relation to what's 'er... the questioning. This may relate to whether you give me reasonable answers to the questions which I put to you. Do you understand that ?'

'I understand that, sir'

'First of all you were arrested by myself at 9-30. Do you know the reason you were arrested ?'

'No.'

'You don't know the reason why you were arrested ?'

'No.'

'You were arrested by myself on suspicion of causing criminal damage to a table.' Canton waited for George to answer. He was warming up the interview slowly but George wasn't playing. 'Do you understand now why you've been arrested ?'

'I understand why you say I've been arrested.'

'Do you understand now why you've been arrested ?'

'No.'

'I've just told you. You've been arrested for causing

criminal damage.'

'I understand why you said I've been arrested. But I don't understand that.'

'The allegation is that you caused damage to a table in the Four Bars public house.'

'I deny that.'

'OK, then... um. Where have you been this evening ?'

'I've been to the Four Bars.'

'And who did you go there with ?'

'Mr Sean Dent.'

'And what relation is Sean to you ?'

'He is no relation.'

'Is he a friend ?'

'Yes.'

'How long have you known him ?'

'Two years.'

'And whereabouts does he live ?'

'He lives in Grangetown.'

'So what was the occasion you were going out for this evening ?'

'The occasion for the night out was the jazz being played in the Four Bars.'

'Did you manage to see the jazz ?'

'We listened to some of it.'

'And were you drinking in the Four Bars ?'

'I had a pint of beer.'

'And what beer was it ?'

'It was a bitter.'

'How much did you pay for that ?'

'I think the price at the moment is £1-98.'

'How much money did you have on you when you came out ?'

'I probably had about twenty.'

'Twenty pounds ?'

George nodded. Canton leaned closer to the tape recorder.

'I note that the interviewee has just nodded.' He smiled at George.'So you stayed in the Four Bars, drank a pint of beer, just to summarise, and you came out with your friend and what was his name again ?'

'I didn't summarise that.'

'No, I'm summarising that.'

'You can summarise that but I didn't actually say that I had just one pint of beer. Can you say how much I had left when I got into the station please ?'

'No.' Canton stared at George. He had been warned about his sort. They were always very polite but very difficult. He tried to remember the textbook procedure. 'How much did you drink in the Four Bars ? I'm talking about the Four Bars now.'

'I probably drank one pint of beer at a price of about £1-98.'

'Right. So you went to the Four Bars, right ?'

'That is correct, yes.'

'And was Sean with you then ?'

'He was, yes.'

'Exactly what time did you get there ?'

'I have not got an accurate recollection of the exact time.'

'Approximate time then ?'

'Eightish.'

'Did you meet anyone there ?'

'No.'

'How much in total have you drink ?' Canton began to mix up his tenses, 'Have you drunk this evening?'

George turned to his solicitor, 'Can I stop this interview ?' He could feel the heat rising in the questions. 'Is this going ok ?'

'Yes, fine. You're up on points.' Shannon smiled.

Canton challenged him. 'What does that mean ?'

'A technical term.'

Canton scowled at the solicitor. Shannon offered George a rest. 'Is there anything you want to discuss with me in private ?'

George laughed, 'No go on, where were we ?'

'Are you happy to continue this interview ?' Canton directed the question at the duty solicitor.

Mr Shannon waited, then decided he was tired of Canton. 'Yes, I'm perfectly happy.'

'So going back to the Four Bars then, how much did you consume in there in total ?'

'One pint.'

'One pint ? And in total in the evening, how much had you drunk ?'

'One pint.'

'How would you describe your state ?'

'Coherent.'

'How would you describe your state now.'

'Moving towards sobriety. '

'What ?'

'Sobriety.'

Canton looked at George. He was pissing him off. 'Would you say that you were jolly this evening ?'

'No, I would say I was coherent.'

'Would you say you were drunk this evening ?'

'No.'

'You wasn't drunk.'

'I was not drunk.'

'Have you drunk anything else besides that one pint ?'

'I have not.'

'Would you be prepared to take a blood test ?'

'Sure.'

Canton looked at 7084. Where was the rule book ? 7084 had memorized the rule book.

'Okay, so tell me what happened in the Four Bars then ?'

'Do you want all of it ?'

'Yeh fine. You explain it to me.'

'We entered. Bought a drink that lasted for a while. As

long as a drink tends to last. We talked, the jazz started, during the first break Mr Dent decided to go home. I continued to listen to the music on my own when I had a dispute with a gentleman over the ownership of a drink and I was set upon by the bouncer.'

'Okay, so you say you were set upon by the bouncer. In what way did he set upon you ?'

'I believe he knocked me over from behind and in the course of that I may have knocked my head on a table, leaving me temporarily unconscious.'

'For the purpose of the tape can you confirm that you are wearing a black leather jacket, a stripey beige and black shirt, blue jeans, brown walking boots with black laces ?'

'Red laces.'

'What ?'

'The laces are red. They might look dark but it's the...'

'Yes, okay, red laces. Is that a fair assumption of what you are wearing ?'

'Yes, I would say that.'

Canton stalled, there was a point about the boots he wanted to make but he couldn't rememeber what it was. He went back to his facts. 'When we came along and I arrested you, I placed hand-cuffs on you because you were being restrained. Information that I had received suggested that you were violent.'

'That was incorrect. I was not violent. I was asking for the police at that time.'

George looked at Canton. They both knew he was getting nowhere but Canton wasn't enjoying it. 7084 Andrews decided it was his turn to come in from the cold and join the fun. He spoke with a fading Scottish accent that gave his voice a juvenile lilt he was desperately trying to lose.

'In the Four Bars. What was the atmosphere like in there?'

'Ragged.'

'And you say you went there about nine o'clock?'

'I think I said eightish.'

'Did anything out of the ordinary happen?'

'No.'

'Just you and your mate. Any other mates?'

'Not that I can recall.'

'Basically the two of you having a drink, would that be right?'

'Yeh, we're slow drinkers.'

'A drink, a chat, sat by yourselves?'

'Yeh, plenty of room on a Saturday night.'

'Were you mixing with anyone else apart from your friend Mr Dent?'

'No.'

'Had there been any hassle in there?'

'No.'

'Right, but for no apparent reason you were set upon.'

'I told you, I was having a minor disagreement with these two men in front of me over the rising cost of admission and

I was set upon.'

'What two men ?'

'I don't know.' George began to realise that the police knew as much about the two men as he did. He'd struck lucky, hitting the two people in the club who obviously had good reasons not to go offering statements to the police on a Saturday night.

Canton kept his eyes pinned on George but 7084 was struggling.

George steadied himself to make another denial when his unobtrusive solicitor decided to speak again.

'Can I just make a comment at this point ? So far we've had Mr Rees giving his explanation but no specific allegation has been put to him at all. I think it is only fair that the allegation is put to him so he can answer it.'

'Can I just finish my line of questioning first ?'

'I don't think you should be allowed to put any more questions to him until you put the allegation to him as to why he's in this interview.'

'Ok, if that's the way you want to play it.'

Canton weighed in again. 'Don't quote me but I'm not sure if I put an allegation to him at the start with regards to what the allegation...'

'All you said to him was do you know why you're here ? You didn't actually say that an allegation has been made, that is, X,Y & Z.' Shannon was sharper than his eyes suggested.

'Right. Three witnesses that were inside the public house, not doormen, state that you smashed a table inside the pub. What can you say about that ?'

'I categorically deny it.'

'Sorry ?' Canton looked incredulously at George.

'I categorically deny it.'

'The first witness stated that you punched an unknown person standing in front of you and then proceeded to pick up a table and smash it on the floor.'

'An unknown person ?'

'Yes, well, we haven't taken a statement from the assaulted man yet but that a man was assaulted can be confirmed by the doorman.'

'Perhaps you ought to find the assaulted man ?'

'Don't tell me what my job is.'

'Why not ? You don't seem to know.' George allowed himself a smile now. He was well clear on points. He could afford some risks.

'I would like to record at this point that the interviewee is being abusive towards me.'

'I dispute that. I'm just offering some friendly advice.'

'Mr Rees, I would advise against this.' Shannon wanted to go home now.

George stretched a smile across his face and waited. But 7084 tried again.

'Why do you think these witnesses would approach us in the first place ?'

George was ready with an answer but Shannon was quicker. He turned to the policemen, time to pack up. They'd had their chance.

'I think Mr Rees would find it impossible to answer that question. He doesn't know what's going on in their minds.'

'That's a question I would like to ask.'

'It is not a question that would be allowed in court. It's inadmissible.' Shannon turned to George. 'I don't think you should answer that, Mr Rees.'

'I would like to concur with my solicitor.'

Andrews ploughed on. 'Why... er of all the people in that... have been in that pub today. Tens of customers, would the bouncer jump, attack you ?'

'I can't answer that. I have no idea.'

'You can't answer it ?

'I don't think it is a relevant question I can be expected to answer.'

7084 looked at Canton. They were all going nowhere.

'Right, can you just confirm that the form that I explained earlier, form F325. That I've given you that form.'

George hesitated, squinting at the form but Canton's patience had gone.

'It says F325 in the top right-hand corner,' he shouted, his finger stabbing viciously at the paper.

'I'm just reading it, that's all.' George winked at him. Canton stood up sharply but 7084 caught his shoulder, holding him. Shannon looked up at the PC and raised his eyebrows. George didn't move. Canton walked back towards the door, swearing quietly to himself.

7084 continued. 'Is there any representation you want to make ?'

George looked at Shannon.

'It's a standard form, Mr Rees'

George shook his head. He signed the form.

'You hold that. It's for your purposes. Is there anything you wish to say with regard to what you've spoken about.'

'Nothing whatsoever.'

'Have you understood everything we have spoken about?'

'I have. Yes.'

'The time by my watch is 23. 33. The date is still Saturday the 17th of October. I am stopping the tape.'

xi

The night was still flowing as the desk-sergeant let him out of the front entrance to the station.

'Let's not see you again, George.'

He pulled his coat collar up and headed down the steps. The sergeant shook his head sadly. Perhaps he should have kept him in until morning. There was something in the man's controlled intensity that worried him. He had seen it before but couldn't remember where. There was only so much you could do. He had no record. A complete blank, without even a minor caution or a d&d. There was nothing on him. He was employed by the city as a care worker and that was it. No driving licence, no credit cards. He wasn't on the electoral roll, but then half of the people in the flats on Cathedral Road had no past to remember. People could just drop out. He could continue walking and they'd never see him again.

He watched him merge with the people still flowing out from the city. They should have kept him in.

George waved down the first taxi that blinked empty. The driver peered dubiously out from his cab.

'Where you going ?'

'City Road.'

He shook his head then opened the door.

George relaxed into the soft seats as the taxi spun around on the wide street. Other lights cut into the car. Then the click of the road as the vehicle speeded up and ran the first amber light.

'Busy night, no ?'

George looked up at the grinning face of the man in the mirror.

'Could say that, mate.'

'Town very busy tonight. A lot of people want to go home. Very noisy people. One of them sick over my car last night. Very rude people. I tell you this drinking business no good for people, no good at all.'

George allowed the words to fill the spaces in the car. Three sets of light later the driver pulled a sharp left.

'How far ?'

'By the garage.'

The taxi slowed to a halt, illuminated by the bright neon of a garage forecourt.

'That's three-fifty.'

George passed four coins to the man.

'Keep it.'

'Thank you, sir.'

He pushed himself out of the car and walked further into the light of the garage. The lights stung his eyes, colouring the edges in bright reds where the vision smudged into primary. He brushed his coat down and checked his face for fresh blood. He was clean. He walked up to the cashier who was shielded from the night by a glass plate and a metal counter.

'Can I have a petrol can, please ? My car's broken down.'

The boy looked bored as he quickly scanned George up and down before pushing himself down from his seat and walking further into the darkened store. He quickly came back to the window.

'Do you want petrol to go in it ?'

George nodded.

'How much ?'

'How much does it hold ?'

'About a fiver.'

'I'll have five pounds of petrol then, please, and a box of matches.'

The boy touched the numbers into the till. 'Right, that'll be nine-fifty-eight.'

George passed a ten-pound note under the grill.

The boy rang the purchase before pushing himself off his seat again and heading for the door. George was waiting for him.

'Pump four.'

He took the plastic petrol can, the matches, his change and headed for the pump. He guessed this was going to be easy.

♦ ♦ ♦

George tripped the security light as he vaulted the padlocked gate into the yard. The light bathed the empty car-park. No one moved. George huddled under the wall. He knew it would go off. The wind set it off on bad nights. No one noticed.

George could just make out the words Team Headquarters, before the light clicked off again.

He skirted the wall and fiddled with his keys for the Yale he was looking for. It went in easy, the door pushing back into the darkness before the dull insistent sound of the warning bleep on the alarm was cut by the numbers seven, eight and four which George pushed into the keyboard. He didn't need the police yet.

The reception led off into the darkness where other rooms flanked onto a wide corridor. One room would be enough. It would all go.

The swash of fluid on the carpet fell quietly around the room, its thick promising smell easing up into the air. Waiting. The can emptied easily, then clattered into the far corner. A match flared brilliantly in the darkness before exploding as it hit the carpet. The flash of petrol igniting burst out through the window, searing into the night. George reeled back from the heat, smiling, his face lined by heat and tears as he watched it burn.

xii

'P c's okay, Sean ?'
He looked up at Kaite then at the café sign, then
back to Kaite.

'Okay ?'

Sean nodded.

'You manage the wheelchair ?'

He nodded again.

Kaite pushed open the door of the café holding it for
Sean, who manoeuvred Andy and his wheelchair over the
metal lip of the threshold.

A man in the corner looked over the top of his *Daily
Mirror,* noting the entrance, then returning to his fag and a
story on a big transfer for a Manchester United player. A
dark woman with three children peered out of the window,
looking bored. She didn't even turn round as Kaite moved a
seat so that Sean could wheel Andy's chair to an empty table.

'Tea ?'

Sean nodded.

'Tea, Andy ?' His head spun around, face full of a smile,
then looked over the rest of the cafe which was
disappointingly empty. Andy liked crowds.

'What you'll 'ave, love ?' A thin woman, her hair tied severely back, old before fifty, took the order.

'Three teas.'

'The weather's been bad. Wind.'

Kaite smiled.

'I'm in an attic flat.'

'Don't know how you do it, love.' She passed three cups of bubbling tea across the counter.

Kaite returned to the table.

'Thanks, Kaite.'

'I'll let it cool for you, Andy.' Andy was unconcerned, everyone always let it cool for him. He continued watching the café, focusing on the occasional blur of a person passing in the street beyond.

Sean watched his tea, then drank it. He was quiet. But it was a Friday afternoon. He was due to visit his father on a Friday afternoon. He liked visiting his father, but not every Friday afternoon.

Kaite picked a battered paperback out of her bag. She would have been hard pressed to remember the title of the one she had read a week ago. People always raved about books, kept them on shelves like treasured objects. The cover of her present reading material was bright orange and came with a claim that seventeen million people had read it. She had tried to imagine that number of people but was left thinking of whole cities. She could remember a couple of books, moments for her, fragments of their stories but only in pieces. They were for reading and then moving on.

She waited for the afternoon to wash away.

It drifted on. Like a hundred other afternoons on Corporation Road. Mothers pushing babies, children winding their way home from school. Cars stuttering along, frustrated by lights and the big orange double deckers which roamed the city swallowing then disgorging passengers. Kaite dreamed her way through twenty pages, Sean drank three cups of tea, Andy watched the mothers, babies, children and buses flow past the big steamed window of PC's. He watched the old man who sold the *Echo* on the corner of the junction protected by railings and smothered in fumes, his hands smudged black with ink from yesterdays news. The headline board promised, 'My life with the body-in-the-bags murderer'.

Towards four, Kaite finished a chapter, Sean finished another cup and between them they pushed Andy home.

xiii

A ndy's house warmed up quickly with the three electric rungs on the fire driving away an edge to the November air that had settled over the city. Soon the fogs would creep up from the Channel, clothing everything in a dirty white shroud that hid the people from the sun. The fog liked the city and would stay and hug its new friend for weeks as it thickened with each new flush of commuter traffic.

Andy settled comfortably in front of the television, content to be home with people he liked. Kaite switched from her novel to a magazine plucked from a pile under the coffee table. Sean sat at the window staring out through the venetian blinds, waiting.

'Do you want a drink, Sean ?'

Sean turned from the window; he appeared unsure of the question; turning it over in his mind.

'No ?'

He shook his head.

'I'll just get one for Andy.'

She pushed herself reluctantly from the settee, casually checking the clock on the wall. Another hour before Mike would arrive. They were supposed to be inducting a new worker next week. Another face for Andy and Sean.

Sean returned to view the road while the deliberate repeated sounds of Kaite making tea filtered in from the kitchen. He turned around when she came back with Andy's plastic beaker. She bent down to give Andy the drink when Sean offered to help.

'Can I do that for him, Kaite?'

'Yeh, sure you can.' She handed him the beaker.

Sean sat on the armchair next to Andy and began to give him his tea. Andy didn't appear to notice it was Sean but merely tipped his head back as the tea was offered.

'I feel sorry for Andy.'

Kaite was reading a magazine article .

'Do you, Sean ?'

'Yes, I do. I wish he could drink the tea on his own.' He thought his words over, then added hurriedly, 'I don't mind doing it for him though. I just know he'd love to do it for himself.'

She looked up from her reading. 'Yes, he would, but you mustn't think like that, Andy's happy enough, he wouldn't like you thinking that. He doesn't want you to feel sorry for him, he enjoys his life.'

'But I do.'

'Yes, but.' She searched for an answer. 'I know you do.'

Sean looked at Andy, who smiled at him.

'I'm sorry, Andy. I know I shouldn't but I do, you don't mind, do you ? I like living here. I wouldn't like it if I have to leave, you don't mind me living here, do you ? You don't, do you, Andy ? You and me are going to be friends, aren't we Andy ? You'll like me. I'm good, I am. I'll be your friend.'

Andy looked at Sean, aware he was being spoken to. His head spiralled away in laughter then stopped and stared back at Sean.

'I'm going to see my Dad tonight, Andy. He's lonely, see. You don't mind me going, do you ? Perhaps you can come with me one weekend.'

Sean continued to offer Andy his drink but his friend's head spun away. Sean turned back to face Kaite.

'George isn't coming tonight, is he ?'

'No, he won't be coming tonight.' She cursed under her breath. She'd been assured that Angel had explained everything to him.

'Will he be coming tomorrow night ?'

'No, I don't think so.'

'Angel said he might not be coming again. Is that true, Kaite ? Why is that true, Kaite ? It's not true, is it ?'

Kaite placed her magazine down carefully.

'I don't think he'll be coming again, Sean.'

'Why is that ?'

She tried for the words but didn't answer. Sean turned back to Andy.

'I always lose my friends I do, Andy. I don't know why, but they leave me. My mother's gone, she's in heaven. I can't see her until I go there. I don't want to go there yet. I'm not allowed to see Sarah any more and George has gone. You knew George, didn't you, Andy ? He's great George is, me and him do the papers.' He paused, turning his sounds over, finding a question for Kaite but then burying it. 'Never mind, you and me, Andy, we'll be friends.' He looked at Andy beaming. Andy again spun his head away, laughing, but swallowed it sharply as a loud blast from a car horn blustered in from the street.

'Taxi ?'

Sean peered out of the window and nodded.

'Got all your stuff ?'

Sean pointed to a sports bag with Adidas written on the side next to the doorway.

'Say hello to your Dad for me and Andy. And enjoy yourself at the football.'

She stood up from the new settee in time to give him a quick kiss on the side of his cheek.

'See you, Andy.'

♦ ♦ ♦

Ebisu

Sean is watching a screen. A screen that flickeres out to him, bathing his face in splinters of black and white. The screen speaks to him; words and phrases, whole sentences break their way through a vision of static. The lights suggest shapes. Light fingers, pressing. Moving shapes, figures of people just behind the blurred curtain of black and white. Laughter stirs from the street beyond.

A discarded wrap of chip paper stained with grease and red sauce lies on the carpet. A mug of tea cools by the side of a chair.

Sean stares into a screen of static listening to the words that reach out and touch him, phrases, whole sentences, shadows moving behind the splintered curtain of black and white.

♦ ♦ ♦

xiv

Rain slithered down the grease-smeared pane, tracing lines through the trees, black posts to the park, stripped taut against the squall that had drifted in from the Channel.

The wind knocked twice on the window as a sharp eddy twisted its way up and out of the bare, brushed yard. George stirred from his bed. A hidden afternoon sun directed his gaze across the littered floor to the window.

He could see out through a gap in Teilo Street, beyond the slated roofs to where a line of horse-chestnuts marked the edge of the park. In spring they were always the first trees in the city to offer leaves to the new year. They flushed quickly with a sharp, hopeful green which deepened through the summer until, with the turn of the big tides which flooded up the river, they would conspire, paint themselves a watered orange, watch the retreating daylight and then, with the first sharp November storm, undress overnight, and George would know another year had slipped forward.

He pushed himself out of bed. A warm damp smell caught his nose as he sat on the edge of his mattress. It was a smell of sweat and beer, pubs, smoke and cheap food. The fetid smell of a late, last night. It was the smell of George, and its rancorous presence repelled and reminded him. His face grimaced at the roll of fat which bulged unevenly around his stomach. It was the only spare weight he carried but it was growing. He hung his head forward before shaking it, then winced with the pain as the reaction thudded into him.

He looked around for his clock which was not where it should have been, perched on the bookshelf above his desk, tucked into the far corner of the room. The flat was covered with a fall of papers and clothes which meshed together, obscuring the boards. An upturned chair pointed its legs upwards. Closer to the window a neat row of cups and plates shared the draining board with a blue kettle in an isolated protest against the general disorder of the room.

George struggled forward to the sink. He turned the water on, grasping handfuls of it as he attempted to hydrate his flooded and drained body. He waited to climb out of the trough. A stained shaving-mirror hung above the sink, his dark, sunken eyes stared out at him.

You show me a mirror. I do not always like what I see.

He kicked over a few papers in a desultory search for the clock. He guessed early afternoon. Time moved slowly on a Sunday.

He needed food and a shower. Sunday afternoons were not the best time to find the bathroom empty. Mrs Dia on the ground floor would usually embark on her mission to pickle herself at two and could be still submerged and singing by five. He couldn't understand how she managed to keep the water warm. When he risked a bath the grumbling boiler would release a ration of tepid water that only just lathered the soap.

Sunday evening used to be chapel with Andy. They both enjoyed the singing. There was not much point in going alone. He didn't find he had much to do lately, Sunday or the week. Still, he needed to be clean. He hoped it was early enough to beat Dia to the water.

xv

Kaite put her magazine into her bag on the side of the settee. The clock ticked on.   'Almost   six   now, Andy. Mike will be here at six.'

Andy turned away from the tv screen.

'You usually see George on a Sunday, don't you ?'

Andy's face cracked into a smile and his throat made a light gargling noise.

'George isn't coming tonight, Andy.' She looked closely for comprehension but Andy continued smiling, unperturbed by the information. Kaite looked away, out toward the window and the drawn venetian blinds.

'Never mind, perhaps Mike will take you out instead ?' adding, as if to apologise, 'and at least you won't have to go to that chapel any more.'

Andy returned to the television. He knew what Kaite's voice sounded like. It was part of his safe world.

'At least you won't have to go to that bloody chapel. All that singing with the minister ranting on about forgiveness. What's he got to forgive you for ? Never did a bit of harm to anyone, did you, and what's he got to say about that ? Nothing at all, pats your head at the end of the evening and thanks you for coming. God's will and all that, only he can't convince himself, never mind about anyone else. Bloody wonderful. I don't know why George ever took you.'

Kaite looked desperately at Andy, as if this time he would have to answer, but she knew he would ignore her. She turned away defeated.

'Sean will be back tomorrow.' Andy turned immediately at the mention of another name, a name which cut a smile for Kaite.

'He's deserted you this weekend, hasn't he ? Gone to visit his father, still it's nice to have some peace around here again isn't it ? He's all questions Sean, doesn't stop, does he ? You like him though, don't you ? He's a lovely lad really.' She paused and Andy again drifted away to his partner in the corner.

'You don't mind him living here, do you ?' Her voice wandered. 'He's got to have somewhere to live, and his father can't have him all the time, so he's living here with you. You don't mind, do you, Andy ? You'll be good friends, you'll see.'

She pushed herself up from the settee and walked over to Andy. She leaned to kiss him but stopped. Andy looked up. Kaite was crying. She wiped tears from her eyes. Her thoughts were cut by the notes of the doorbell. Kaite walked briskly out of the room. Andy turned to the noise and slipped lower into his armchair.

Sounds of a brief cold greeting drifted in from the passageway before Mike appeared in the doorway. He was a tall man who gave the appearance of being stretched as he peered down from beyond his gold-rimmed moon-glasses. Strangers had mistaken him for Andy's brother, sharing the same emaciated arms and legs that hid under ill-fitting shirts and jeans.

Andy's face fired in a breach of enthusiasm as Mike lifted his arms in greeting before bounding over to where Andy is sitting. His head swung buoyantly from side to side as he dredged up sounds which spun out into a high pitched giggle.

'How's my boy been, aye ?' Mike's voice climbed to match the energy of his entrance. 'What you been up to ? Been out on the town, 'ave you ?' He waited confidently for a response, winking furiously at Andy before continuing, 'Tell you what, what about me and you popping down The Packet for a pint tonight ? How's that then ? Lovely.'

Andy began another cackle of laughter as his hand came up from his side to frantically brush his nose. It subsided but he had slipped further down into his chair.

'You've slipped down there, Andrew, let me help you up.' Mike stooped to loosen the belt, then pulled Andy up. Andy's torso bowed out in a reflex action which he held for a second before relaxing back into the chair. The whole process of lifting was performed with an ease that understood the routine.

'There you are, Andrew. You shouldn't slip down like that, you naughty lad. Stand up mun, it's better for you.'

Andy's eyes followed Mike avidly as he crossed the room

to fetch a chair from underneath the window. Mike sat down and stared expectantly at Andy, his eyes waiting for the words that would not come. As Kaite returned to the room they both looked away. Mike with relief, Andy to a new distraction.

'Do you want a cup of tea, Mike ?'

'Good idea, put one on for Andrew here as well.' His voice was now ironed with a flat normality as if in relief from the effort of its previous incarnation.

'He just had one.'

'Never mind, he'll have another one with me.' He turned to address Andy as his first voice prepared to jump from its box. 'Won't you Andrew boy ?'

Andy twisted his head back towards Mike.

'Course you will, proper teapot, aren't you ? Just like your grandmother used to be, aye ?'

Andy continued to smile at Mike, confident that he was going to receive something.

Kaite handed Mike two mugs of pale tea.

'Thanks, love, you're a darling.' Kaite's face tightened as he thanked her but it washed easily over him. 'There you are, Andrew, I'll put it there a minute, let it cool down a bit.'

He took a quick swig from his mug before turning to Kaite. His voice again subsided to a flat normality.

'How's he been ?'

Kaite returned to the far side of the settee so their speech jumped across Andy, who followed the sounds as they talked.

'He's been okay, we had a walk down to the pier this afternoon. He got a bit cold in the end though, didn't you, Andy ?'

'How's his movements been ?'

'Not very good. Might have to get a new prescription for him.'

Andy was unconcerned. It was Sunday evening, soon he would be going out.

'I'll change him now. Quick change and you'll be all set for tea.' His voice slipped effortlessly between its two incarnations as if the only communication Andy was able to understand was loud and enthusiastic exhortations.

A tight silence drifted uncomfortably into the room as the people who could speak thought of something more to say. Mike took a drink from his tea, Kaite glanced at the screen. The pictures moved.

'I guess you heard about George ?' Her voice was heavy with resignation. She had already discussed George with Angel, Hilary and Sean. Mike was the only one left.

'He's had it then ?'

'Looks like it.'

'Poor bastard, I never thought he'd do something like that.'

'Nobody else can either.'

'Guess he's not too popular with the Team.'

'Not too popular with anybody, I think.' Kaite had liked

George. He had made her laugh in his rare, unintentional way. She had once asked him to stay the night with her in a barren flat off the Corporation Road. He had accepted shyly but let himself out before the sun had climbed above the factories in the morning. She sometimes wondered why he never returned; it hadn't been that bad, but whenever she tried to turn the conversation to a personal level he managed to drift away to easier, more mundane topics.

'Any reason for it ?'

Kaite merely shrugged her shoulders.

'Guess they'll drag up his past.'

'They'll have to.'

'How's Sean taking it ?' A delicate tone of inquisition had settled over Mike's voice.

'He was upset.' She paused, searching for the correct explanation. 'He couldn't understand it really, he thought it was something to do with him but he didn't know what.'

'And no bugger would tell him.'

Kaite looked at Mike but offered no further words.

'Who's going to do the papers with him ?'

'Nobody, as far as I know. I think we'll have to drop it unless of course you...'

'I would of course but my back's not what it was.'

'Really ? I thought you were swimming again.'

'Therapy.'

Kaite suppressed a smile. Mike took his back very seriously.

'Never mind, it's only fifteen quid.'

'Always thought he was getting ripped off.'

'It was only that much because George used to chip in extra out of his own pocket.'

'The daft bugger. Did he really ?'

'From the start apparently.'

'Still, it's not as if it was a proper job or anything.'

Kaite looked away. She knew it was more than the job to Sean.

'He'll get over it.' Mike paused while he assessed the new developments in the ever changing service to himself. 'He'll bloody have to, I s'pose. It's a shame about George though, he wasn't a bad old bloke. A bit deep, if you get my drift, and we didn't always see eye to eye. That's right, Andrew ? Too right we didn't. But you can't see eye to eye with everyone, can you, Kaite ?'

Kaite raised her eyebrows but knew from experience that any subtlety in communication with Mike was hopeless. He only understood one language.

'Never mind, Andrew. I'll take you out tonight, alright mate ?' He pushed Andy's arm jovially with his fist, jolting him sharply from his communion with the screen. Mike stared at him, making wild eyes from behind his glasses. It was a performance Kaite had found amusing the first time but tonight she was tired of the house and a long vacant Sunday afternoon.

'I've got to be going, I'm off out tonight.' She was lying

but it came easy now. Mike had a habit of enquiring about her life that annoyed her intensely. He could see no reason why 'an attractive girl like herself,' as he had often reminded her, 'was still not married' Mike had a talent for ignoring the obvious, but she knew it was not obvious to Mike. Very little was. She knew he didn't mean any harm and seemed incapable of thinking anything negative about her or indeed anyone, but the reason she would have given would have stretched his reserves of good feeling to the limit. She simply, except for extremely rare occurrences, didn't like men. Not personally, but physically: their presence of complete self-absorption, and the unquiet assumption that she should need them. It was easier to live alone and take lovers.

'Out on the town, aye Kaite ?' His eyes sparkled as he saw an opportunity to increase his knowledge of Kaite's life. A life that was frustratingly elusive.'Going with someone special ? A new man perhaps ?'

Kaite simply stared at him, hoping her eyes were as aggressive as she felt.

'No ? Never mind, one will turn up.'

Kaite looked at him with increasing disbelief.

She picked her leather bag from the side of the settee before striding over to Andy. One day she would get through to Mike, but it wasn't going to be today.

'See you then, Andy.' Andy looked up as Kaite bent over and kissed him lightly on the top of his head.

'Have a good night then.'

She smiled thinly at Mike before heading for the doorway. Mike counted slowly to himself before the door slammed as he reached four.

'Right then, time to get sorted.' His voice still held its effusive edge but gradually faded in fervour as he began to address himself.

'It's just me and you now, u'are 'ave some tea.' He picked up the adapted mug from the table and inserted it into the side of Andy's mouth.

'Where shall we go tonight then, Andy ? Down The Packet, is it ? I tell you what, we'll go to The Packet, see a few of your old mates, what about that ? We won't bother with the chapel, you don't want to go down and listen to that old singing, do you ?' He waited briefly for an answer. 'No, I thought not. Couple of pints down the pub and we'll pop back and catch the snooker, you'll enjoy that, won't you ?' He looked away at the screen, then up at the clock, which had faded unnoticed past six. His wife would be still at her mothers. The boys would be on their own.

'Anyway, finish your tea.' He allowed Andy the opportunity of one more swallow before he put the mug back on the coffee-table and removed the now sodden towel which he had left around Andy's neck as a bib.

'C'mon then, Andy.' He stood up and leaned over to unbuckle the belt at his waist.'There you are, Andy, quick change.'

He struggled with Andy's weight as he crabbed across

the room and out into the corridor towards the bedroom beyond.

xvi

Collins ticked a long line of figures in his account book, then checked the total on a calculator which flashed a new number for him to disagree with. Thursday afternoons were always slow. Mrs Betts had been in for her daily pack of Regals; the Whitbread rep had been due at two but, as usual, was late. A handful of other faces lingered, fingering his magazine rack before buying a paper. A dosser from the bridge on the river bought a bottle of 'Bow. Steady, slow trade on the dead end of November. He tried once more with the figures, but his brain refused to concentrate. He needed a break, a week in the Canaries, but he couldn't afford to go until at least the end of January, probably February. Two more months. He could never fully convince himself that the time-share had been a good buy. When he was there - black sand, warm sea, cheap spirits - the packed shop on Corporation Road was another world away. But he could never get the weeks he wanted, met too many Germans and the service charges were higher than he expected. Re-sale was out of the question; the figures he'd been quoted, he might as well have given it away. Two more months.

The door of his shop flicked open, tripping the welcome

if irregular sound of a paying customer. Collins looked up hopefully. His smile faded as Sean beamed back at him.

'Hello, Mr Collins.' The big clumsy lad ambled over to the counter.

'Sean ?'

'Come for my papers, Mr Collins.'

Collins studied his face closely. A big, smiling, open, honest face. A woman had rung from the Council on Tuesday explaining that Sean and George would have to give up the round. She had mentioned something about George resigning.

Collins put his pen down.

'Where's George ?'

Sean just shrugged.

'Thought you'd given it up ?'

'No, not me, Mr Collins. I'm here.'

Collins frowned deeply. He didn't like problems.

'Where were you last week ?'

'I was ill, Mr Collins.'

'Really.' Collins shuffled a stack of newspapers.

'Very ill, Mr Collins.'

'And George ?'

'Dunno.'

'Someone rang about George. He's given it up and you can't do it without him.'

'No, me, Mr Collins. I'm here.' Sean tried hard to stick to his lines.

'On your own ?'

'I know the houses, honest I do, Mr Collins. The Embankment and the flats.'

'Well, I'm not sure, all these papers.'

'Please, Mr Collins I got to do it.' Sean held his empty sack up with one hand.

'Need the money, do you, son ?'

Sean nodded.

'Got a girl, 'ave you ?'

'Yes, Mr Collins.'

'Expensive things, son.'

'She pays sometimes, Mr Collins.'

'Got a good one there then.'

'Or her mother does.'

'Even better.'

'I'm saving, Mr Collins.'

'Oh yeh. What for ?' Collins looked down at the stack of papers. Time was getting on.

'We're going to London.'

'Bloody waste of money that, son. I can tell you.'

'And other things.' The smile began to fade on Sean's face.

'Yeh, I'm sure.' Collins glanced down to his figures, hoping they would provide the answer. Why couldn't things be simple ? But then he had been unable to find anyone to take over the round and he hadn't been looking forward to doing it himself again. It was cold for November and warm in the shop. 'Ah, what the hell, you want it, you can do it.'

'I'll do it right, Mr Collins.'

'How many papers you usually take ?'

'Er, papers. George usually does the numbers, Mr Collins but...'

Collins began counting the papers. 'How many streets is it ?'

'It's the Embankment and the Gardens.'

'That's thirty-nine the Embankment. Twenty-three for the Gardens, nine for the Close. And the flats take twelve. That's er...'

'That's...' Sean struggled with the figures.

'Here's hundred.' Collins decided he never could count. 'That should cover it.'

'Right, Mr Collins. I'll do it right through. All the houses.'

'Yes, I'm sure.' Collins pushed the papers over to Sean who placed them in his bag.

'Got them, Mr Collins.'

'What you waiting for then ?'

'Nothing. I'm going to do them. Thanks, Mr Collins.'

Reviews for *My Piece of Happiness*

"Proof that high quality fiction is being published within Wales. The book is a sensitive exploration of the relationship between a series of handicapped adults and their social worker, George Rees...Among the most impressive things in the book for me is the way Lewis Davies manages to write convincingly about mental handicaps without ever making those handicaps explicit. It is a triumph of careful and sensitive writing." Mario Basini, *The Western Mail*

"It has integrity. The anger, outrage, frustration is finely honed and does not tip over into diatribe or cynicism. The simplicity of the prose is deceptive, its effect admirable. A well-crafted novel that manages to be uplifting." *Scrawl*

"The book was very moving but also extremely witty. I laughed out loud at the discussions that took place in some of the meetings. It made a fairly train grim journey to London a lot more pleasurable." Julian Hallet, Down's Syndrome Association.

"...wry and understated but charged with a muted lyricism."

Cambrensis

"Despite imperfections this is a brave work, hovering occasionally on the edge of brilliance." Glenda Beagan, *Planet*